The Hill: Finding The Way

Book 3

Wayne James Coleman

Wayne James Coleman

The Hill: Finding the Way

Copyright © 2025 by Wayne James Coleman

All rights reserved

All Rights Reserved. No part of this publication may be reproduced, stored in a retrieval system, or transmitted, in any form or by any means, electronic, mechanical, photocopying, recording, or otherwise, without the written permission of the Author.

40 Cutter Mills Rd #405, Great Neck, NY 11021

Dedication

To my family, friends, and readers who have encouraged me along the way. This story is as much yours as it is mine, for each of us is on a journey of finding the way.

Acknowledgment

To you, reader—thank you for walking this journey with me. These stories lift us beyond the ordinary, revealing the mystery and gift of the divine, if we dare to believe. Writing them has been a reflection of my heart, my questions, and my trust in Christ. He is near in our stumbles, our victories, and in the quiet moments when we wonder which path to take.

"If something is worth having, it is worth waiting for." We may not always understand what God is doing, but we can always trust Him." These truths capture the mystery and character of the three books in this series. Without Christ, none of this would have meaning. May these pages encourage you, challenge you, and remind you that God walks with you every step of the way.

Contents

Preface

Welcome Back To The Hill

From its very beginning, The Hill was a real sacred place—a place of wonder and discovery. As a boy, I discovered my Hill, and that sense of awe has never left me, even in moments when it seemed hidden. It lingers quietly in the heart, waiting for us to recognize it again, calling us to pause, reflect, and listen. The wonder and discovery of the Hill do not need to end; it teaches us that it is never too late to turn, to seek, and to find what our hearts long for.

The Hill reflects the joys, questions, and choices of those who walk its paths. For returning readers, it will feel familiar, yet it holds new insights waiting to be uncovered. For first-time visitors, to fully experience the depth of the story, it is best to read the books in order:

1. The Hill: The Journey Begins
2. The Hill: Seasons of the Heart
3. The Hill: Finding the Way

Writing these books has been more than setting words to paper—it has been a journey of the heart. Along the way, I recognized myself in the hopes, struggles, and prayers of the characters. This third book feels especially close, for the decisions faced here are ones we all encounter at some point in life.

At its heart, this story is about listening for God's voice in the quiet places, choosing trust when the way forward is uncertain, and finding courage to walk on in faith and love. I hope that as you follow Derek's path, you'll also catch a glimpse of your own.

And as Pastor Roberts might gently remind us, for those who find themselves in the later seasons of life, may there always be wisdom to share, encouragement to offer, and a quiet strength to pass on.

So come—step once more onto the Hill. May you find a part of your own story here. Let its quiet awe remind you that even when hidden, God's presence is near, guiding each step. Listen closely, for the Hill calls to every heart—its invitation is personal, and it waits for each of us to come and discover what God has prepared. And perhaps, if the Lord allows, there may yet be more stories to tell.

Chapter 1

When The Noise Becomes Personal

"Noise can drown out truth, but sometimes it awakens something deeper. Not every storm outside is meant to be silent – some are meant to stir the soul." — reflection.

"I lift up my eyes to the hills—where does my help come from? My help comes from the LORD, the Maker of heaven and earth." — Psalm 121:1–2

A woman stood beside him at the elevator, earbuds in, head slightly bobbing to something only she could hear. She didn't even glance his way as he pressed the button. Derek Callahan couldn't block out the noise even if he wanted to.

The blare of a siren a few blocks away. A TV is shouting behind a half-open apartment door. The distant sound of protest echoed through the concrete streets below. But he needed to stay aware. Perhaps it was his military training, or the hours spent in the woods with his grandfather, learning to listen to the subtle sounds of leaves, wind, and each distinct bird's call. To sense the world quietly, deeply, even when others ignored it. You never turned out everything, not completely.

The elevator arrived. Derek stepped in with the lady, but he felt alone. Twelve floors up, he entered his apartment, dropping his keys on the counter, and walked straight to the balcony. The city looked different from up here—still and somewhat quiet, waiting to be understood.

Derek stood still, arms crossed, eyes scanning the horizon like he used to do on base. At 29, he carried the weight of things most men his age hadn't yet faced — former Army intelligence, trained to anticipate threats, read between the lines, and solve problems before they erupted. But this? This uncertainty, which seemed to affect everyone, was global. Many try to ignore it.

He wasn't dealing with a code or an enemy. He was trying to decode a world unraveling in slow motion. Uprisings in Spain, Germany, Paris, the UK, and many other places. He didn't know it. He was trying to make sense of his life. Everyone he talked to was going on with life. What other choice did they have? Life felt unsettling.

At 5'10", he stood shorter than both his father and grandfather, but height had never been his measure. His presence came from clarity. From instinct. From the way he walked into a room and saw what others missed. But lately, even clarity seemed clouded. At twenty-nine, he felt he had experienced more than he wished he had.

The world was changing. Fast. Violently. What was once considered wrong is now right, and what was right is now wrong.

Quakes, floods, firestorms, like the earth itself, had begun to groan. Derek had paid little attention to prophecy before. Too many people use it as a tool of fear or distraction. But now…it felt like the headlines were pointing to something more profound. Even Christians who had previously dismissed the noise as just another cycle were watching more closely. Anxious. Unsure.

And what hit Derek hardest wasn't just the chaos out there, but the loss of something steady. The values of his grandparents, which are now considered outdated by many, are used to make the person feel less intelligent if they disagree. Derek admired his grandfather, who often quoted a Bible verse that speaks of God as the same yesterday, today, and forevermore. He still believed in God. At least, he thought he did, not like his grandparents. God seemed to be their life. For him, God took a backseat. Not rejected. Just neglected. His phone rang, breaking the silence.

Nancy.

He let it ring.

Not now.

They'd been seeing each other for a year. Long enough for questions to surface. At 27, Nancy was attractive, sharp, confident, and about 5'5". She worked for one of the major news networks—the kind of outlet Derek rarely trusted anymore. She was good at what she did—driven and persuasive.

Maybe too persuasive.

They were opposites in more ways than one, and lately, they seemed to argue a lot. She leaned liberal. Twisting facts into compelling narratives was part of the job, but Derek couldn't always tell where the reporting ended, and her beliefs began. She once told him, "Truth is whatever you need it to be." She hadn't been raised in faith. Her parents had split when she was a teenager, and after college, she never looked back. Her mother's choice of men was something she didn't want for herself. Marriage meant nothing to her, just a piece of paper and tradition; it guarantees nothing. But lately, she'd started pushing the idea that they should move in together.

Derek wasn't sure why it made him uneasy. Nancy was fun and smart, and they did get along well, that is, if they avoided certain topics, such as religion and politics. Perhaps that was the tension under the surface—something unspoken that wouldn't settle.

Derek's grandfather Dirk's voice often echoed in his mind:

"If anything's worth having, it's worth waiting for."

"And know the difference between feelings and truth. They don't always go hand in hand." Derek remembered that his grandmother, Melissa, always said, "Don't forget—be equally yoked." You cannot build a home if the foundation is not solid.

One of her very last words to him was, "It wasn't just about compatibility, Derek; it was about beliefs — direction."

And something about Nancy, for all her charm, felt misaligned—like a beautiful road headed the wrong way.

His phone rang again.

He sighed, this time answering. "Hey. Hey, Derek. I'm sorry. I won't be able to make it for dinner. I'm chasing something downtown—could be big". He nodded to himself; "Okay" was his response, and he wasn't sure why he felt a sense of satisfaction saying that.

A pause on Derek's part. Then she said, "Derek, we need to talk about us.' I mean, really. I brought up moving in, and you just kind of shut down. Are you even serious about this relationship?"

The silence at his end stretched too long.

He wanted to say yes. But something—deep, quiet, immovable—held him back.

"Nancy", he began slowly, "I care about you. A lot. But I don't want to rush something that I'm not sure is right."

"You're not sure I'm right?" She asked with an edge.

"No, that is not what I mean. I'm just…" Derek exhaled. Trying to figure out what this is. "What we're building. If we're building the same thing."

She jumps in and says, "It's that marriage thing, isn't it?" she said, sharper now. "You're still holding onto that old script. Perhaps you feel moving in would be a slippery slope. You want a ceremony and a contract before anything real happens."

There was a bite in her tone, though she tried to rein it in. "I'm just saying," she added, a little calmer now, "people don't need paper to prove their commitment. You either know or you don't. And if you're still unsure, perhaps you've already answered your own question."

"Nancy, it's not about a contract," Derek responds sharply.

"Then what is it about?"

Derek opened his mouth, but nothing came. After a beat, she said, "Look. I've got to go. Let's talk at lunch tomorrow, okay?"

"Yeah," he said quietly. "Lunch. Okay. Be safe."

"You too."

The line went dead, but her words lingered. Derek turned and walked to the kitchen, still unsettled. He needed something to do with his hands. Bread. Mustard. Turkey. He began making a sandwich, as muscle memory took over where clarity had left off. He sits down on the chesterfield, and still lingering are the words, "It's the marriage thing, isn't it?" she'd said, her voice now cooler, like a shade had been drawn. Derek slipped the phone onto the counter, staring at it for a long moment. Twelve months. That's how long they'd been together. Long enough to know a few things. Long enough to realize he still didn't know if they were building the same thing. He ran his hand through his hair and let out a breath. He couldn't even explain the knot in his gut. Was it her views on truth? On faith? The way she spoke so casually about moving in, like commitment was just a convenience?

Something in him felt off—disconnected. He couldn't remember the last time he felt grounded. Not in a relationship. Not even in his own life. His grandfather Derek used to say, "If you're unsettled, don't ignore it. That's most likely God trying to get your attention. And you know what to do."

Derek didn't know. But then, from out of nowhere came—

The Hill.

That place where everything used to make sense. Where the noise faded, and the silence didn't feel empty. Derek used to pray there as a boy. Really pray. Trust. Listen.

But it had been so long.

So much has happened.

Then, almost without thinking, a verse surfaced from memory like a whisper breaking through fog: "I lift up my eyes to the hills—where does my help come from? My help comes from the Lord, the Maker of heaven and earth."

He blinked. Where did that come from? He hadn't thought about that verse in years. His grandfather had often quoted it, especially when things felt uncertain. Maybe it wasn't just a memory. Maybe it was a reminder. Derek wasn't sure if he even knew how to connect anymore. God, who once felt so present through his grandparents, now seemed like a distant figure lost in the shuffle of life and too many goodbyes. His grandfather would say, "God doesn't slip away—you just stop turning your head. You can talk to Him anytime."

Derek sank into the arms of the couch and closed his eyes.

"God…" he whispered.

Silence.

He tried again, but the words felt foreign in his mouth, like speaking a language he hadn't used in years. His throat tightened. How do you pray again, when you're not even sure who's listening? Or maybe listening is the problem. It's the awkwardness.

He opened his eyes with a sigh. "Guess life took over."

That's when the verse came. Unbidden. "I lift up my eyes unto the hills." He didn't even notice he had clicked on the TV for background noise. A news anchor appeared, her voice low and serious. The red banner scrolled across the bottom: Breaking: Multi-vehicle collision on Interstate 15. Road rage incident suspected. Several dead. Dozens injured.

The Hill: Finding The Way

He froze.

His chest tightened. The sound of the fridge humming behind him seemed to stretch into eternity. A vehicle accident. Road rage. Just like before. His mind went back—uninvited—to that day.

His parents. His grandparents. All four. Gone. Some idiot with a temper had run a red light, chased another driver, and had torn into the side of their van. They'd been on their way to the Hill. Grandfather had a new Hill. He wanted to show the spot to Derek's parents. Make a day of it. Picnic. Prayer. A return to something sacred.

They never made it.

Derek hadn't either. He was still overseas. He prayed as if he had never prayed before, and not only did his prayers fail, but he arrived too late. Everything felt distant. He wondered where God was. Perhaps that is when everything changed. His ache is still there. He looked down at the sandwich in his hand. Everything felt distant. The food. The room. His life.

The verse "I lift my eyes unto the hills" seemed to wait to be answered. Derek didn't finish the sandwich. Appetite gone, he left the plate on the counter, turned off the TV, and wandered to his room. The shadows on the walls seemed deeper than usual.

He lay on the bed and stared at the ceiling, his body still, his mind far from still.

That verse still lingered. "I lift my eyes to the hills…"

His eyes finally closed.

The Dream.

The dream came without warning. No slow drift. No gentle entry. One moment, Derek lay in bed; the next, he was standing not just in a dream but in it. The air was thick and humming, charged with a tension that buzzed beneath your skin. There was no wind, no sound. Nothing guided me. Yet I was being led. Pulled forward by something unseen, unmistakable. There was a sense that something was about to happen.

And then it came—a massive arm descending from the void above. Not threatening. Not human. Mighty. Righteous. Ancient.

Its finger stretched forward, commanding.

"Look.

See.

Time is near."

I caught my breath, and I could feel it as a lump in my throat. The world split open before my eyes like torn fabric, and I was in it. A woman clothed as if she were in the sun cried out in labor, agony etched on her face. A crown of twelve stars shimmered above her head. Above her loomed a great red dragon. Its breath was so foul I tried to cover my nose and mouth lest I vomit from the stench. Seven heads twisting, eyes glowing, scanning with ancient malice. It waited, ready to devour. The scene turned with violent suddenness.

War.

The sky above ignited with light and flame. Armies of angels clashed with forces of darkness, their weapons blazing, their cries shaking the heavens. A name rang out like thunder—"Michael." And then the dragon was cast down. I stumbled as the earth reeled beneath my feet. I saw cities split by violence. Fires rising. Streets filled with hatred. Chaos spread like ink in water. Everything blurred—rushing images of protest, flags, children weeping, men and women shouting words of kill. Then I saw churches full, but empty, as if the spirit that had once been there had been removed. Then there were many being baptized, weeping with joy. Then I heard the words: "Come, the time is close." But outside of this was noise. Not a noise of joy but of lostness.

Truth was drowned in noise. I wanted to scream, to run, but I could only watch. Everywhere I turned, people grasped at comfort like a lifeline, choosing ease over truth, lies over conviction. And behind it all, behind polished smiles and self-justified slogans, I saw the dragon still working—not subtly as he used to; he felt he had to twist and was in a desperate hurry to complete his work.

A voice called out from above,

"There will be a time of distress such as has not happened from the beginning of nations until now" (Daniel 12).

I turned and saw people praying, faces upward, desperate, but their prayers hit a barrier. They didn't rise. They faded, tangled in confusion. The words were before my eyes. The Prince of Persia stood up to me.

Prayers were being blocked. The false beliefs and sin seemed to make them fall to the ground before they could reach their destination. People believed what made them feel good, even if it was convenient, even if it cost them everything real. Right and wrong blurred. Up became down. God became offensive. Evil became celebrated.

My chest ached. I cried out, but no sound came. Then, through the smoke and rain, I saw it—

The Hill.

Small, steady. Untouched.

And kneeling on that Hill, a multitude of faces in tears, hands lifted, voices trembling but clear. Their prayers rose like threads of light. The darkness trembled. The dragon recoiled. And the unseen hand pointed again.

"Time is near."

Derek awoke with a jolt. He sat up in bed, heart racing, shirt soaked with sweat. The room lightened as dawn crept in. The dream—the vision—lay vivid on Derek's mind.

The woman.

The dragon.

The battle.

The confusion.

The hate.

The Hill.

Derek whispered almost involuntarily, "Jesus…what are you trying to tell me?"

Derek sat on the edge of the bed, the room still cloaked in a predawn gray. The dream, if that's what it had been, clung to him like a damp fog. His heart was still pounding. His hands were clammy. He buried his face in them. It had felt real. Too real.

The hand…the voice…the dragon…The Hill.

Without thinking, his hand reached for the phone on his nightstand. Grandfather Dirk. He had to tell him. He always knew what to say. His thumb hovered over the screen and then stopped. The contact was still there. But he wasn't. The ache hit him like a sudden drop. His hand lowered, phone still in it. He stared at it in silence.

"What am I doing?" he cried, his voice feeling hollow. He dropped the phone back down. In a realization, he felt alone. The weight of absence settled on him heavily, more real than ever. Derek stood and began pacing, the floor cold beneath his bare feet. He couldn't shake the images—flames in the sky, the woman crying out, confusion thick as smoke blanketing the earth. He needed to talk to someone. But who? Not Nancy. She wouldn't understand—not this. She would try to listen. He thought of calling her anyway, just to hear her voice. But something held him back. A memory. His grandfather's voice, steady and clear, rising from somewhere deep in his heart:

"Don't cast your pearls before swine, Derek. That's what Jesus said. Matthew 7:6. Some things are too holy for the wrong ears."

Derek had always bristled a little when his grandfather quoted that verse. It sounded harsh. But Grandfather never said it with harshness, only with reverence, like the truth that carried weight. And maybe that's what this was. Not a moment to explain. A moment to listen.

Derek stops, looks up, and says, "God, what do I do with this? What are you trying to tell me?"

Derek sat still, the phone still resting on his lap, the room dim and quiet around him. His thoughts circled back again and again to the dream—the war, the voices, the broken world. And the Hill. He didn't understand it, but he knew what he had to do. He picked up the phone, opened his travel app, and booked the earliest flight he could find. He was going home.

Not just to a place.

To a calling.

To his Hill.

Chapter 2

Going Home

"There are places where God met us once, and sometimes, He draws us back not to relive the past, but to awaken the future." — Reflection.

"Stand at the crossroads and look; ask for the ancient Paths, ask where the good way is, and walk in it, and You will find rest for your souls." – Jeremiah 6:16

Derek stood by the bed, his suitcase open but half empty, just like his thoughts. He moved slowly—shirts, jeans, a light jacket—folding more out of habit than intent. It wasn't just clothes he was packing. He was carrying questions, restlessness, a weight he couldn't quite name.

His phone buzzed. A reminder to call Nancy.

He sat on the edge of the bed and stared at the screen. What was he going to tell her?

He tapped her number.

"Hey," she answered quickly, warmth in her voice.

"I didn't expect to hear from you so soon."

"I'm heading home," he said.

A pause. "Home? What's going on?"

"I just… I need time to think."

Another silence, longer this time.

"It's about us?" Nancy finally asked, voice tight.

Derek looked at the floor, questioning himself. "No. Not really. This isn't about us. At least, I don't think it is. I just know I need to go."

There was a pause. Then she sighed—sharp and wounded. "You don't think it is about us? That's not much comfort, Derek."

She crossed her arms, stepping back slightly. "You say you need to go, but you can't even explain why. And now I'm supposed to be okay with that?"

"Nancy, I'm not trying to push you away," he said, his voice low.

"But you are," she snapped. "You're pulling back and leaving me to just sit here wondering what this means. You won't even tell me what's going on."

Derek swallowed hard. "It's complicated, Nancy. I'm not trying to push you away."

"But you are!" she snapped. "And now everything's complicated? That's what people say when they're looking for the exit."

Derek clenched his jaw. "It was a dream, okay," and after saying it, he wished he hadn't.

A beat of silence.

"A dream?" Nancy's voice cracked with disbelief. "You're leaving because of a dream?"

Derek winced. "Look, I didn't mean it like that. It's just— my grandfather always told me—"

"Oh," she interrupted, her tone turning cold. "So now it's a vision?"

He paused. "I told you… you wouldn't understand."

A heavy silence.

Then she said flatly, "God, Derek. I think maybe we need a break."

His heart sank. "Nancy—"

But just then, the buzz of his phone interrupted.

"That's my Uber," he said quickly, trying to steady his voice. "We'll talk soon."

"Sure," she said, and the call ended.

Derek sat for a second, phone still in hand, already regretting mentioning the dream. He slipped it into his pocket, stood up, and grabbed his bag. As he stepped outside in the city air and into the Uber, his grandfather's voice came back like a whisper from long ago: "The world will shake, Derek—but never forget, God keeps His promises." He then would quote a verse: "Let us hold unswervingly to the hope we profess, for He who promised is faithful." My grandfather always had me repeat the verses after him.

The Airplane.

Derek sank into his window seat and buckled in, the hum of the engines barely cutting through the weight in his mind. As the plane lifted off the tarmac, climbing into the clouds, his thoughts drifted back not just to the dream but to his grandfather's voice echoing through memory.

"The Bible is centered on Israel, Derek. Every page speaks of them, for it was through them that the law, the prophets, and the Messiah came. Even when they drifted from God, as they have now, He has not forgotten His promise." He could still see his grandfather's aging hand holding his Bible and tapping the scripture verse gently. "For the gifts and the calling of God are irrevocable" (Romans 11:29). "They are the timepiece. Watch them, and you'll understand the times. Though most of Israel doesn't see Jesus as the Messiah yet, one day they will. But not without suffering first."

Derek stared out the window as the clouds rolled by. The chaos he had seen in his dream—the nations pulled like puppets, the dragon stirring unrest—it was all wrapped around the land of promise. Somehow, the madness on earth still circled back to Israel, like it always had. From the moment Abraham first walked the land, the battle had never ceased.

Derek whispered to himself, more prayer than thought. "Lord, help me see what this all means."

But the ache in his chest lingered—Nancy's words, sharp and final, still hung in the air like smoke that wouldn't clear. He hadn't meant to hurt her. He just couldn't explain something he barely understood himself.

There was only one thing he knew with certainty: he had to go home.

The plane touched down with a jolt. After collecting his bag and renting a car, Derek sat behind the wheel for a long moment. The silence pressed in.

"Now what, Lord?"

The Hill: Finding The Way

The Hill.

He drove slowly through familiar roads, each turn stirring a childhood memory. The fields rolled out on either side, just as they had when he was a boy, though the fences looked newer, the trees older, more tired. He slowed, letting the rhythm of the tires carry him back. Derek could almost feel his grandfather's steady hand on his shoulder the first time he introduced him to his Hill. Derek could almost hear the call of the meadowlarks cutting across the summer air.

Finally, he turned onto the lane he knew by heart—the one that had led to his Hill. The place where he and his cousin Jennifer had played and laughed. The place where he first met God. No sounds, no thunder, but a gentle calling in the wind.

But as the car crested the rise, his chest tightened. His breath caught.

The Hill—his Hill—was gone. In its place stood a neat row of identical houses, squared against the sky, their manicured lawns and trimmed hedges leaving no trace of what once was. A subdivision, ordinary and soulless.

Derek pulled the car to the side of the road. For a long moment, he sat motionless, hands gripping the wheel, as though letting go would sever the last thread that bound him to the past.

Finally, he stepped out, the air sharp in his lungs. He turned in a slow circle, searching for something, anything that reminded him of his boyhood sanctuary.

"What now?" he whispered.

Everything had changed.

Everything. "How could I be so wrong?"

"Nancy was right." The words slipped out before he could stop them. "All of this is foolishness. Dreams. Nostalgia, nothing more."

He reached for his phone, thumb hovering over her name. He would tell her she was right, that it was just a foolish dream, a passing emotion. That he'd be on the next flight back. He almost tapped call—but paused.

He got back in the car, his hand still resting on his phone, as a gentle breeze drifted through the open car window. It carried with it a soft scent of lavender, which was strangely comforting. The late afternoon sun broke through a cloud, lighting the cracked pavement with a golden hue that caught his breath. For a moment, he froze, and his grandfather's voice came to him, low and steady, telling him, "Lavender," he said, "was the scent of God's nearness. When it comes, Derek, pay attention. It means you're not alone."

Derek closed his eyes, allowing the scent to fill his chest. The subdivision, the loss, the years between—it all didn't seem so heavy; it all seemed to fade beneath that lingering fragrance, as if heaven itself had leaned close to whisper.

He looked up, drawn from his thoughts by the sound of footsteps on the gravel.

An older woman, perhaps in her seventies, was approaching with a slow but steady gait with a golden retriever by her side. She stopped just outside his window, her eyes clear and knowing.

"Young man," she said, tilting her head slightly, "you looked troubled."

Derek was about to brush it off, say he was fine. But the words stalled in his throat. After everything he'd just seen—or not seen—it wasn't far from the truth. Nancy had been right, he'd told himself. All of this was foolishness.

"I thought I'd find something here," he muttered.

She nodded thoughtfully, not pressing for more. "Come, walk with me."

Derek hesitated. He glanced at his phone, thinking of calling Nancy, of telling her she was right and he'd been wrong.

But instead, he slid the phone into his pocket. "Sure," he said, "why not?" He was not even sure why he had said that. He got out of his car and walked with her.

They walked in silence for a few moments. Her golden retriever trotted beside her, nose to the path. The woman's pace was steady but unhurried; her presence calming. Her presence was actually what Derek needed: peace and calm. He asked her if she smelled the lavender; she just smiled.

Derek said, "I don't know what heaven smells like, but it must be this."

"I'm Althea," she said as they rounded a bend.

"Unusual name," Derek replied.

She smiled. "It means healer… or more deeply, one who brings direction. My mother hoped I'd live up to it." She gave a light chuckle.

"I'm Derek. I was named after my grandfather, Derek, so we share a similar name, but each of us is different."

"I know," she said, almost as an afterthought.

Derek glanced sideways at her, puzzled. "You d…o?"

She didn't elaborate. Instead, she nodded toward a couple wandering ahead of them, their movements uncertain, turning and hesitating at each fork.

"They don't know where they're going," she said softly. "Most people don't. Do you?"

Derek didn't answer.

They continued until they came beneath a magnificent tree, its limbs stretching wide above the path. Althea slowly raised her hand, pointing to the highest branch.

"Do you see him?"

Derek squinted upward. An eagle was perched at the top, still and steady, its eyes sharp and fixed.

"Look how he watches," she said. "Nothing escapes his eye. He doesn't fidget or panic. He just sits—assured, strong. If people would take the time, they could learn a lot from him."

She let the thought settle before continuing.

"Eagles show up in Scripture often. Majestic. Strong. Able to endure hardship. Isaiah 40:31 says, 'But those who wait on the Lord renew their strength; they shall mount up with wings like eagles.' That's no accident. Eagles endure storms. They rise above them." She continued, her voice low, assured with wisdom as if someone who walked the path of life. "And came through stronger. Psalm 103:5 says, 'He satisfies us with good things so that our youth is renewed like the eagle's.' And in Exodus 19:4, God says, 'I carried you on eagle's wings and brought you to myself.'"

"You see," she said, "God is often compared to the eagle—majestic, faithful, strong, like the eagle that bonds for life. God bonds with His children and cares for them. In Exodus 19:4, God says, 'I carried you on eagle's wings and brought you to myself.'"

Derek said nothing, but thought, this lady sure seems to know her Bible. He was glad he had agreed to go for a walk.

Althea turned back towards the tree. "But the problem isn't that God isn't speaking—it's that we don't take the time to see, listen, or watch. I've had plenty of time to learn that."

Althea turned slightly and extended her hand. A soft hum rose in the air as a hummingbird hovered just above her open palm. Its wings shimmered, beating with a speed and stillness that seemed impossible.

Derek stared. "How did you…?"

She smiled. "They come when you slow down enough to notice."

He watched in silence.

"You see this little one?" she said. "It's one of God's masterpieces. It can fly forward and backward—no other bird does that. Its wings beat up to 80 times a second, yet it can stop and hover long enough to enjoy the sweetness of what God provides. So many people rush, trying to get somewhere. But this one…this one teaches us to be still, to savor, to go back if needed."

She looked at Derek again. "There is much we can learn from the hummingbird, Derek. And just like the Hill—it isn't gone. It's still here; it just looks different. It's what it taught you. What it still calls you to remember. You just need to look closer. You need to look beyond the noise. Beyond what society tries to cover. It doesn't even know it's covering it up."

The hummingbird hovered a moment longer, its wings a blur of delicate power. Then, with a shimmer of green and gold, it vanished into the trees. Derek stared after it, stunned.

"That was…unreal," he whispered.

Althea smiled gently. "Sometimes God uses small wonders to shake us awake."

Althea looked directly at Derek and unexpectedly said, "You have a relationship problem," matter-of-fact.

Derek blinked. "What?"

She turned towards him, once again, eyes calm but piercing. "You're carrying something unresolved. It's right there in your spirit."

He sighed. "Yeah… my girlfriend doesn't believe in marriage. She says it's just a piece of paper. She wants us to move in together."

Althea tilted her head. "Derek, is this temporary?" As if to say, you are not seriously considering it.

Derek hesitated. "No, at least not to me."

Althea, with a warm concern in her voice, asked, "What about children? What message are you giving them if you treat something God made sacred as if it's optional?"

"We haven't really talked about kids. That's farther down the road."

They walked a little farther in silence. The golden retriever padded ahead, then circled back and waited beside a worn wooden bench beneath a maple tree, its canopy casting dappled shade over the path.

Althea gestured. "Let's sit. This discussion will take some time."

They sat. The dog settled quietly at her feet.

Derek looked down at his hands. "She's not a bad person."

"I know," Althea said gently. "But even good people can fall for bad lies. And the Bible reminds us—we're all flawed. There is no one righteous, not even one. That's why we need God's truth to guide us, not just our feelings."

Derek nodded slowly. "You know that my grandfather Derek once told me about his first wife, Jenny. She wouldn't even date him at first. Said they'd be unequally yoked—he wasn't committed to Christ. She had strong convictions. After she died of cancer, he eventually married my grandmother, Melissa. Both ladies would say that if something is worth having, it's worth waiting for, and we must distinguish between feelings and truth. I think I'm finally beginning to understand."

Althea nodded. "That kind of wisdom doesn't die with time—it grows deeper with it. Feeling may start the journey, but only truth keeps you on the path. Those ladies are wise."

"I know Jenny and Melissa well."

"You knew my grandmother?" Althea smiles.

She rose from the bench, brushing her skirt smooth. "Well…my job is done here."

Derek looked up, puzzled. "What do you mean?"

"Don't linger," she said with a soft, knowing smile. "Pastor Roberts is waiting for you."

Derek had a surprised look on his face. "You know my great-grandfather?"

"He's waiting for you?" Derek's head snapped toward her.

"I know him very well," she said, smiling gently. "He lives in Bethany Bridge Senior Living. He's been waiting for you, Derek. And truth be told, we've been waiting for him, too."

Derek, more puzzled than ever, asked, "What do you mean—many are waiting for him?"

Althea's expression grew stiller. "His time is drawing near. Those who've gone before him are waiting. And those still here—some don't even know it—but they're waiting for what only he can give before he goes."

Derek felt the ground shift beneath the conversation, something stirring beneath the surface.

Althea turned towards the trees.

"Hurry now. Time is short."

She began to walk away. As she moved down the path into the trees, Derek stood as to follow, but she raised her hand. "You can't go where I'm going," she said without turning back. "It's not your time."

Derek stopped, puzzled, watching as she walked further into the trees. The scent of lavender lingered in the air, mingling with the last golden flickers of sunlight filtering through the leaves. Then she was gone—vanished into the path as if absorbed by the light itself.

Derek stood there for a long moment, the quiet pressing around him. Something had shifted—something deep.

And now…someone was waiting.

Chapter 3

Where the Past Waits to Speak

"Sometimes the answers we need aren't new—they're waiting in the voices of those who came before us. The past still speaks, if we're willing to listen." – Reflection.

"This is what the Lord says: Stand at the crossroads and look; ask for the ancient paths where the good way is, and walk in it, and you will find rest for your souls." – Jeremiah 6:16 (NIV).

The glass doors slid open with a soft whoosh as Derek stepped into the nursing home lobby. A faint scent of daisies sitting on the desk added to the warm, welcoming smile of the woman sitting at the desk. Soft music played from a speaker near the receptionist's desk as a few residents shuffled past in wheelchairs and walkers, nodding at Derek.

Derek gave his name at the desk and stated that he was there to visit his great-grandfather, Roberts.

The receptionist said, "You must be speaking of Pastor Roberts; he is a darling, a ray of sunshine."

Derek smiled and said, "Yes. If any of us has a problem, we go to Pastor Roberts. He may be 99, but his wisdom is still sharp."

The receptionist pointed down the hall. "Take the second left."

He asks about Althea, but no one mentions her. No one seemed to know her.

As Derek walks down the hallway, the scent of daisies seems to disappear, and a scent of antiseptic and fresh cleaning takes its place. He pauses at the open door and sees Roberts sitting in a comfortable recliner with an open Bible on his lap. He hadn't seen his great-grandfather for years. After the funeral, that was when he was still in the military.

As Derek stands at the doorway, Pastor Roberts looks up and says, "Come in, and close the door so we can have some privacy. Everybody knows when my door is shut, not to come in," and he chuckles.

Pastor Roberts said, "You came. I knew you would be here today."

Derek smiles, figuring Althea must have told him that they were talking. He stopped for a light lunch before coming.

Derek crossed the room without hesitation and wrapped his arms around the frail man by the window.

"Sorry, great-grandfather, for not coming sooner," Derek said softly.

Pastor Roberts holds him a few moments longer and then extends his arms, saying, "Let me take a good look at you. You remind me of your grandfather, Derek."

"You have come about a dream."

Derek's brow furrowed. "Yes…how did you know? I didn't even know I was coming until today."

The old man gave a faint, knowing smile. "Your grandfather, Derek, told me you would come. My daughter, Melissa, your grandmother, and your grandfather, Derek, told me the day before they left on their outing with your parents. He said someday you would come to me with a dream."

"I think he knew something was going to happen."

A shadow passed over Derek's face. "If he knew something was going to happen, why would he go?" His tone sharpened, the buried pain and confusion edging into his words before he even realized it. "Why would he even go?"

Pastor Roberts nodded slowly, eyes filled with quiet understanding. "How much your grandfather truly knew, only he and God can answer that question. But I know this: he wouldn't hide away from spending time with your father out of fear."

Derek's expression tightened as the ache surfaced again.

He believed, Pastor Roberts continued, like the Psalmist declared, that "the Lord orders the steps of a good man." Dirk trusted that even when it made little sense. He knew we don't always understand what happens in life…but he also believed God could always be trusted.

Derek looked down, jaw clenched, that old anger stirring again. Pastor Roberts watched him carefully.

"I saw it in you when we first spoke," he said gently. "The anger was not just directed at what had happened, but also at God. You've tried to bury it. Stifle it. But it's shaped how you've seen Him—or not seen Him—all these years. You're hurt, Derek. I know, because I was hurt too."

Derek looked up at him, surprised.

"I was living with them, you know," Pastor Roberts continued. "After Melissa's mother passed away, they insisted I move in. I was with them. And then I came here."

Pastor Roberts looks down at the open Bible on his lap. "I wasn't going to stop trusting my Savior after all these years. We live in a world where bad things happen, and they're only going to get worse. That doesn't change who God is. And if we want to understand why the world is broken in this way, we only have to go back to the very first story."

"You went to your Hill looking for something. You knew that something was missing in your life. Maybe you're hoping to revive what you had as a kid. When you were on that Hill, you experienced God."

"Your grandfather wrestled, too. When he lost Jenny, it nearly crushed him. He poured it all into his journals. You should read them. And maybe talk to your uncle Greg. He walked through that valley with your grandfather. He would be excited to see you."

"That reminds me, your grandfather gave me something to hold for you." He gestured to the dresser in the corner. "Bottom drawer. There's a large sealed envelope."

Derek moved to the dresser, knelt, and opened the drawer. Inside was an aged, large manila envelope, thick and sealed, labeled "The Hill."

Derek walks back and takes a seat in front of Pastor Roberts. He broke the seal and drew out four journals.

Each journal was carefully labeled in Derek's tidy handwriting:

1.   The Hill: Where the Journey Began.

2.   The Hill: Seasons of the Heart.

3.   The Hill: Finding the Way.

4.   The Hill: The Choice Within.

The third journal was titled but contained nothing. The fourth was titled, and once again, nothing was written. Derek opened it—and found the pages blank. His eyes lifted, puzzled.

"He gave me two with titles only."

Pastor Roberts looked up, unsurprised. "Those journals—your grandfather wrote every word. You'll find some very interesting stories in them. Reflections. Lessons. Warnings. Helpful advice and prayers."

Derek nodded as he thumbed through the first journal pages. "But the last two," he said, still holding the blank pages, "I guess he didn't get around to writing in them."

Pastor Roberts smiled, and his eyes gleamed with quiet understanding. "No, Derek. He knew exactly what he was doing. The third and fourth journals are yours to write. It's your stories."

Derek quickly responded, "I don't have a story."

Pastor Roberts smiled and said, "Oh my boy, everyone has a story."

Derek frowned with uncertainty. "Derek looked puzzled, but Grandfather titled these last two books. That is even stranger."

Great-grandfather Roberts said, "I think as your journey continues, the titles will make sense."

Pastor Roberts leaned back in his chair, his eyes drifting toward the window as memories stirred. "You know," he said quietly, "this isn't the first time someone from your family came to me after a dream."

Derek looked up from the journals.

Pastor Roberts continued, his voice steady but touched with reverence. "The night your grandfather first came to my Church, I already knew someone was coming. God told me a man would walk through those doors. And he did, just after sunset. He was the man God sent to the Bridge the night your grandmother was thinking about taking her life."

Derek's breath caught.

Pastor Roberts gave him a long, gentle look. "Sometimes the Dark One attacks us at our lowest point. Brings confusion and despair. Tries to convince us the story's over, that life isn't worth going on. But God had other plans for your grandmother. And He sent Derek."

Pastor Roberts looked down at the Bible resting on his lap, then up again.

"Another point is that your grandmother's role in life was just as important as your grandfather's. Look at it this way—Aaron had a significant role. Moses said he couldn't do the talking. God gave him Aaron. We hear about Moses. It's Moses that all Sunday school children remember, but he couldn't have done it without Aaron. God puts people in our lives to aid us and help us spread the message."

Derek looked puzzled. "What message is that, great-grandfather?"

"The message is very simple. I am sure you remember that," Derek speaks up, "In John 3:16, 'For God so loved the world that He gave His only Son that whosoever believes in Him will have everlasting life.'"

"That's right, Derek."

"Your grandfather was full of life. I can still see Dirk standing in my office when we first spoke. Trouble was written all over him. He'd been having dreams—a vivid one—from the

Bible. The four horsemen. He didn't understand it, but he knew it meant something. That dream lit a fire in him. And began a season of awakening among pastors across the region. Men began to speak again about prophecy and truth."

He nodded toward the journals. "That was the beginning of it all. I figured Dirk knew you would come too—with a dream of your own."

Derek sat back, the weight of the journals in his hands now matched by the weight in his chest. The pages weren't just family history. It was a call. And the third and fourth books—blank— were waiting for him to answer. But the one that interested him most was the one titled "The Hill: Finding the Way."

"He knew it was your story. The fourth one, I'm not sure? He always talked about me writing my story. I will not be writing."

Derek stared down at the blank titled journal, running his hand over the untouched pages.

"Grandmother never talked much about the Bridge," he said quietly. "But whenever it was mentioned, she would glance at grandfather. Her eyes would light up. And then she'd whisper, 'Thank you, Jesus, for sending my Dirk.'"

Pastor Roberts smiled and nodded slowly, his gaze far away.

"Your grandmother was in a terrible state in those days." Pastor Roberts' voice was touched with sorrow and reverence. "Her mother and I did what we could to comfort her. There are wounds only God can tend, so we prayed constantly for her."

Roberts drew a breath. "Her husband, Adam, was stabbed to death and died in her arms. Just a senseless, cruel act of robbery. They were only married for two years, and she was three months pregnant."

Derek's chest tightened.

"She lost the baby a few days later," Pastor Roberts added gently. "Her grief was a canyon so deep, I wasn't sure she'd ever climb out."

Pastor Roberts paused, then leaned forward slightly, his tone more intense now.

He continued, "That's the power of darkness the Apostle Paul talks about. We don't wrestle against flesh and blood, Derek. That battle—it's real. That pain she carried? It wasn't merely a tragedy; it was warfare. The enemy loves to strike when we're weakest."

Pastor Roberts gave a small nod, more to himself than to Derek. "Her mother and I stood fast and prayed. We stood in the gap. That is what we are called to do when someone is too weak to do so. That is what Greg and his family did for your grandfather Dirk when he was in that war of grief and heartache. He could not fight on his own. That is when the tide turned for your grandmother and grandfather; people stood in the gap. Never forget that the power of prayer changes everything. God still moves. Still heals. Still speaks. But His people must believe and walk in faith, not just pay lip service to prayer, as if it were a routine or a whisper before meals."

Pastor Roberts let the words hang for a moment.

"Prayer is a gift. A shield. A weapon. Connection to the Father in Heaven. And too many forget that it has been placed in their hands."

"But God wasn't finished with her story. And today…she's rejoicing with the child she never got to hold."

Derek glanced towards the window, blinking back a sudden sting in his eyes. The ache of loss, the mystery of mercy— it all lived in the silence between their words.

Pastor Roberts leaned forward, voice low with conviction. "And God sent Derek to stand on that Bridge not just to rescue her, but to remind the enemy that Jesus writes the last page in every story, not the dark one."

Derek swallowed hard, the truth of it stirring something deep.

Pastor Roberts looked Derek in the eyes. "That dream of yours, Derek, it's from Revelation chapter 12. You're not the first in your family to receive a warning from Scripture. But now more than ever, we need to pay attention."

"Look at our society. The world. The confusion, the chaos, the rebellion—it's not random. The forces of darkness are at work, openly and unashamed."

He sat back, his voice now low and firm.

"The same God who parted the sea and shut the mouths of lions… is still God today. And He's calling His people to remember who they are. Who He is. Never forget that."

Derek leaned forward, elbows on his knees, voice low.

"I'm not the same man I was when I was twelve," he said. "Back then, I believed with all my heart. Simple, childlike faith. Life-changing faith."

Derek shook his head. "But joining the army and then moving to the city—it's like something in me died. God got lost in the shuffle. I do not know exactly when it happened, but I stopped praying. Stopped listening."

He hesitated, then added, "And there's Nancy. She's not a Christian. In fact, she wants nothing to do with it. Says it's all religious hocus-pocus."

Pastor Roberts let out a slow breath, nodding solemnly. "That's not uncommon these days. They either reject Him entirely or make Him fit into what they believe He should be."

He studied Derek's face, then said gently, "You know, your grandfather Dirk's first love—Jenny—had the same worldview as your grandmother Melissa. They refused to date any man who didn't follow the Lord. Faith wasn't just something they kept—it was the very foundation of who they were."

He leaned forward, voice calm but firm. "There's a reason the Bible warns us not to be unequally yoked."

He reached for his Bible beside him and flipped it open. Second Corinthians 6:14: "Do not be unequally yoked with unbelievers. For what partnership has righteousness with lawlessness? Or what fellowship has light with darkness?"

Pastor Roberts looks up at Derek. "Being a Christian isn't just believing. It's following. That's why the early Church wasn't known just as believers—they were called people of the way.

Jesus' way. They lived as He lived. They forgave as He forgave. They loved truth more than comfort. It shaped their entire worldview. You know, Derek, they were not even called Christians until the 3rd century, and then it was hurled as a derogatory word. Today, perhaps the opposite is happening. Many Christians have turned the word Christian into a derogatory word."

He held Derek's gaze.

"When two people have different worldviews, it's like trying to plow a field with two oxen pulling in opposite directions. To make it more modern, it's like hooking two tractors going in opposite directions. One is joined to God's way; the other, to the world's. Instead of moving forward, you tear the ground apart. You fight, you strain. Eventually, the chain breaks."

He let that settle.

"I'm not just finding fault, Derek. I am warning you. If she won't walk the same road, eventually you'll either leave the path or stand alone. That's the burden of being yoked with someone going in the opposite direction."

Derek exhaled sharply and leaned back in his chair, the journals resting on his lap. He ran his hands across the cracked leather cover of the first one, still trying to absorb everything his great-grandfather had said. The story of his grandmother. The rescue on the Bridge. The warnings about being unequally yoked. Prayer. Dreams.

Derek feels conflicted.

"Great-grandfather," Derek began slowly, "I mean no disrespect, but prayer doesn't always give you what you ask for." He glanced out the window, then back down at the journals.

"I know people who prayed their hearts out…and still lost. And honestly? I know Christians who ended up divorced. So what's the point? It's just a chance you take. Maybe that's why Nancy sees no point in marriage; perhaps she's right."

He looked back at Pastor Roberts, the question hanging in the air, not as rebellion but as a tired, sincere cry from someone who had seen too much too soon.

Pastor Roberts didn't rush to answer. He just nodded, his face full of understanding.

"You're right to ask, Derek. Those are fair questions. And you're not the first to wrestle with them." He sat back slightly, voice calm but firm.

"The problem is, most people think prayer is a way to get something from God. And yes, we bring our requests to Him.

That's biblical. But that's not the purpose of prayer. At its heart, prayer is about connection. Relationship. Christ wants a relationship with us."

He placed a hand gently on the Bible beside him.

"We were created to walk with God, Derek. To know Him. That's what was lost in the Garden when Adam and Eve believed the Lie—that they could do life on their own terms, be their own gods. 'I did it My Way,' as the song tells us, is the problem. We do it our way. Look at the world; where has that got us?"

He leaned forward now, eyes steady. "And when we try to live disconnected from the One we were made for, things break. And we try to patch the cracks with other things—money, control, success, other relationships. It's temporary, covering a hole. It's like using duct tape. Might hold for a while. But eventually, it fails. Yes, Christians can get off track; that is why we need our Hill."

Then Pastor Roberts paused as if switching gears.

"Let me ask you this," he said, tapping the armrest. "When a student gets a math problem wrong, does that mean the problem has no solution?"

Derek raised an eyebrow, unsure where he was going.

"Of course it doesn't," Pastor Roberts said. "It just means they didn't follow the right steps. The method's still true. The answer is still there. And the teacher? The teacher's not wrong."

He gave a slight smile.

"God laid down principles for how life works. He gave us a guide. Just because people fail—whether in marriage, prayer, or life—it doesn't mean God is wrong. It just means we're still learning. Still growing. Our hearts are sinful."

He motioned towards the journals in Derek's lap.

"Your grandfather knew this. That's why he wrote so much—not just about what happened, but what mattered."

Then he looked Derek in the eye.

"Prayer. Worship. Studying God's word. It's not about checking boxes. It's about becoming—being shaped into the likeness of Christ. That's what Jesus showed us in Gethsemane. He didn't pray to escape that cross—He prayed to endure it. To discover God's will. Jesus said, 'If there's another way.' But then: 'Not My will, but Yours be done.'"

Derek swallowed hard, feeling the weight of those words.

"Jesus was divine, yes. But He was also human. And as a man, he understood that God's way, though painful, was the right way. Prayer wasn't a tool to escape the cross. It was the strength to face it."

Derek looked down, quiet.

"As for divorce," Pastor Roberts said gently, "there is a lot of hurt, a lot of pain. Yes, Christians still fall. Some drift from God. Some were unequally yoked from the beginning. Some don't understand what a covenant really means. Sometimes there is pain and brokenness we can't always see. No matter the reason, it is never what God wanted. He designed us for unity. For faithfulness. For wholeness. And even when we fall short, He doesn't. His way isn't always easy, but it's the right way. We are all attacked by the dark forces in heavenly places. Satan wants to destroy relationships."

Derek looked down at the journal again. "I guess I've drifted pretty far."

Pastor Roberts reaches over and gently rests his hand on Derek's shoulder. "The point of prayer isn't to avoid suffering. It's to walk through it without losing who you are in Him. Prayer is a relationship."

Just then, a soft knock sounded at the door, and Nurse Jody, as read on her name tag, stepped in, medication in her hand.

"Pastor Roberts," she said with a gentle smile, "don't you think you should rest a bit?"

"I know you care, Jody," he replied kindly, "and I thank you for your concern and kindness. But I have much to do before I go home."

Jody furrowed her brow, a little puzzled. "But this is your home, and we're your family."

Pastor Roberts smiled. "You are my family, and I'm grateful to be a part of this one. But we've talked about this before. This place is just my temporary home. My real home is calling me, and I still have work to do before I leave this one. Besides," he added, eyes twinkling, "I hope one day it'll be your home too. I'll be waiting to greet you."

Jody smiled through glistening eyes. Derek could see her deep affection for his great-grandfather. She walks over and kisses Pastor Roberts' cheek.

"He's the father I never had," she said quietly to Derek. Then, with a warm glance, she added, "Don't stay too long and tire him out."

After Jody left the room, with the gentle click of the door closing behind her, Derek stood and slowly gathered the journals from his lap.

"I should get going," his eyes flicking to the window where the afternoon light slanted in. "I'm heading to my grandparents' home. They left it to me, and I want to check it out, maybe stay a few days before heading back to the big city." He paused, voice softening. "I learned so much today, and for the first time in a long while, my spirit feels more at home. I hope I can come back and see you before I leave."

Pastor Roberts nodded, his eyes warm. "That'll be good. I think there is more we could talk about. Your grandfather Dirk's journals will be a great help and answer many questions for you."

Derek's eyes dropped to the journals. "It still stirred something in me."

"You carry more than questions, Derek," his great-grandfather Roberts said quietly. "There's grief, but also anger."

Derek looked up, startled.

"It's alright," Pastor Roberts said. "You have learned to stifle it and hide it deep, but we never really hide it, as it comes out in many ways. It's there, slowly doing its damage. It takes away any joy and peace. It brings confusion and uncertainty. I saw it in your eyes, your expression. You wonder how a good God could allow so much pain and hurt."

Derek exhaled slowly, caught off guard by the truth of it.

"You're not alone in that," Pastor Roberts continued softly. "Your grandfather wrestled with anger when he lost Jenny. It's in his first journal. You might find pieces of yourself there. I heard your grandfather say many times that we may not always understand what God does, but we can trust Him. And maybe it's time to talk to your uncle Greg; he and your grandfather have been best friends since childhood. He saw and understood things that your father never spoke of to others."

He reached for Derek's hand and held it firmly. "Before you go, let me pray."

Derek bowed his head.

Pastor Roberts' Prayer came slowly and steadily, like rich soil being turned over:

Lord God,

We thank You for sacred spaces—not built by hands, but shaped by Your presence. Derek comes with grief, questions, and hidden confusion. These things do not unsteady you. You welcome them. Meet him in them. Let him know that even unspoken pain is seen by You—and is never wasted. Let him discover the freedom to bring all of himself, to You. Give him the courage to face what he's buried. Speak through these journals. Let him see that the

Hill he seeks is not behind him, but before him, and You are calling him to seek You. Open his eyes, that he may see Jesus.

In Jesus' name, amen.

Derek steps forward and embraces his great-grandfather tightly. "Thank you… for today. This conversation meant more to me than I can say. Talking with you and Althea stirred something in me that will only grow."

Derek's eyes filled with warmth and love.

"Yeah, Althea," great-grandfather,"She said you were expecting me. And that she was expecting you."

Derek frowned. "Still not sure what she meant by that."

Pastor Roberts's expression softened. "Your grandfather, Dirk, had an encounter once. A messenger, an angel, I believe. He wrote about it in his journals. You should read his story. It might help you understand."

Derek looked puzzled but nodded. "Okay, I will."

He turned and walked down the hall. As he reached the front desk, the nurse looked up from her charting.

"Pastor Roberts said you were coming today," she said almost casually. "But we didn't get any call ahead from you, so I didn't give it much thought. However, I should have realized that he seems to know things others don't. He spends a lot of time talking to God," she replied.

Derek stopped in his tracks. "Really, he knew I was coming?"

He gave the nurse his contact information so that he could be called anytime.

As the door closed behind him, he walked slowly to the car. Much had happened today, things he wouldn't have believed if he hadn't experienced them himself.

He had come searching for a sacred place long gone—but somehow, along the way, he had stepped onto the Hill after all. And maybe, just maybe, he was ready to climb it.

Chapter 4

The Bridge of Hope

"Some bridges carry more than footsteps. They carry grief, questions, and fragile prayers. This bridge was not built for escape but for encounters. Where pain once cried out, hope answered softly." – Reflection.

"When you pass through the waters, I will be with you."-- Isaiah 43:2.

As Derek sat in his car, reflecting on his encounter with Althea and his conversation with his great-grandfather Roberts, his gaze drifted to the journals beside him. The sun had already slipped away, and darkness was now stretching across the sky. He had been sitting there far longer than he realized. The weight of the day pressed heavily on him. He had come searching for a sacred place—a place that might finally bring the settling his soul longed for. And though he still didn't know exactly what was missing, he sensed the faint outline of it now. Still, he wondered if he was prepared for what lay ahead.

He didn't start the engine. Instead, he reached for the first journal. Its pages were worn, its handwriting bold and steady. As he read, one entry in particular gripped him. Dirk had written about a dream—a memory, or perhaps a vision. In it, a dark force hovered close as the twelve-year-old boy prayed on a hill. This shadow lingered beside him until an angel of the Lord appeared, driving it away. His grandfather had added a note in the margin: Daniel chapter 10—prayer hindered for three weeks, Michael the archangel battling Satan.

Derek leaned back in his seat, the journal rising and falling on his chest as his breathing slowed. His eyes drifted shut, and at some point he must have slipped into sleep. When he finally stirred, the world outside had settled into a quiet stillness. The sun was gone, and stars had begun to emerge like soft whispers across the night sky.

He glanced again at the journals beside him.

He had planned to drive to his grandparents' home. But as he sat there, something tugged at his heart—firm, yet gentle. A pull that shifted his direction. To Derek, it felt stronger than a simple nudge; it was a deep craving, an ache not in his mind but in his spirit. A longing that demanded to be filled.

He couldn't ignore it.

Something was calling him—not out of curiosity, but out of hunger. And it was leading him somewhere he hadn't expected.

The Bridge.

It wasn't far—just a short distance from his Hill. As a boy, his grandparents had warned him to stay away from the area; the currents were strong, swift, and had taken many lives.

Derek started the engine and followed the pull—not hesitantly, but with a quiet urgency, as though both his feet and his heart had already chosen the path.

Soon, it came into view.

The bridge stood in the fading light—old, still, weathered by time yet unmoved from its place. This was the very spot Pastor Roberts had told him about. The place where Derek's grandmother, Melissa, had once stood, devastated and undone. Her heart had been crushed under the weight of unspeakable loss.

Adam was gone—stabbed and dying in her arms. And with him, the child she carried. Three months pregnant, the trauma had stolen that life as well.

One could only imagine the storm inside her. The grief. The guilt. The confusion. The aching silence of God.

Derek stepped out of the car and walked toward the bridge. Under the darkening sky, it appeared almost ghostly. Wind whispered through the trees below, and the roar of the water rose like voices echoing from another time. He approached the rail. The wind brushed his face as the water surged below—wild, relentless, like voices calling out from another realm.

And in that moment, he felt it.

Two realities clashing. Two battles unfolding.

Above him, the stars spoke of peace and order. Below him, the water cried of chaos and despair. Derek looked down, heart pounding, and remembered what he had just read—the vision of the dark force, the Hill, and the angel who drove it away. He heard Pastor Roberts' voice in his memory: "Our struggle is not against flesh and blood, but against the rulers, against the powers, against the spiritual forces of evil in the heavenly realms."

He could almost see her—his grandmother—standing here, the waters below calling her into their depths. Darkness encroaching. But then another presence arriving—his grandfather Dirk—guided there at the exact moment she needed him, moved by something greater than himself.

Hope had met her here.

And the calling waters had quieted.

As Derek stood at the edge now, he realized something else: this battle still rages in the hearts of people every single day. The killings, the crime, the pain, the anger, the hate. Most never recognize the true fight. Those who don't know Christ don't know the God who rescues—and so they fight alone. Yet even then, God reaches. Pursues. Loves. Even when rejected, He does not relent.

Derek felt grateful. Grateful for a God who battles through the darkness to rescue those standing on the edge.

Maybe that was why he had been drawn here.

Maybe the battle wasn't just something to witness.

Maybe it was something to join.

He lingered longer, watching the churning waters below. As he stared into the chaos, his thoughts turned inward. He thought of his own life—the routines, the noise, waking up each day and filling time with responsibilities and distractions. But for what? Was that really living? Just clocking in hours, piling more onto an already crowded existence?

And what about those who could barely make it through the day? Was that life too?

And the world—fractured, chaotic. Nations unable to find peace. Leaders blaming others, pointing fingers yet never looking inward. Blind to where the real battle lies.

"There has to be more," Derek cried out in frustration to

the heavens above.

A shooting star flashed across the sky—then crossed back in a strange, startling formation. And he remembered what his grandfather Dirk had once told him: "If we look hard enough, the answer will be there."

He remembered, too, that those who came before him— his grandparents, his parents—had believed there was more. They had seen beyond the veil. They had walked through sorrow and still clung to something sacred.

And then he recalled great-grandfather Roberts' words:

"It all began in the Garden. There was purpose, meaning, and life. But Adam and Eve listened to the Lie—the Lie that said there was more without God. That you don't need Him. That you can be like Him."

And suddenly Derek understood.

This bridge had been a place of decision for his grandmother—a sacred crossroads between surrender and survival. And perhaps he had been drawn here not just to understand her pain, but to recognize his own emptiness.

Was he brought home because the sacred had gone missing in his own life?

Was God awakening something he had forgotten he needed?

The craving inside him wasn't merely for meaning.

It was for God Himself—who is meaning.

And for the first time in a long time, Derek didn't silence the ache.

He welcomed it.

He walked back to the car, his hands cold but his heart restless. He opened the door and sank into silence. The keys hung loosely in the ignition, untouched.

He bowed his head.

Jesus… I don't know what to do, he whispered. I don't even know how to pray.

The silence lingered—but it wasn't empty.

Sometimes the ache in our hearts is more than sorrow; it is a call. A gentle pull from God to return to the place where we stopped listening. The bridge between despair and hope is often built by surrender. And surrender doesn't begin with answers. It begins with a name whispered into the quiet—

Jesus.

And though Derek heard nothing more, the words of Scripture seemed to settle over the moment:

"The Lord is near to the brokenhearted and saves the crushed in spirit." -- Psalm 34:18 (ESV).

Chapter 5

Where Dreams and Memories Meet

"In the quiet of familiar places, our past and present converge. Memories remind us of who we are, while dreams point toward who we are becoming." — Reflection

"For I know the plans I have for you," declares the Lord. plans to prosper you and not to harm you, plans to give you a hope and a future." – Jeremiah 29:11

Derek pulled into the driveway of what had once been his grandparents' home. When he shut off the engine, the world seemed to fall quiet with it. He stepped out, retrieved his luggage from the trunk, and approached the front door. The house key felt heavier than he remembered, and sliding it into the lock felt strangely surreal, as if he were stepping into someone else's memories.

The door creaked open.

He flipped on the lights and closed the door behind him. The air carried the faint scent of old wood mixed with a lingering trace of lemon cleaner. Only then did he realize he hadn't eaten all day. He considered calling for pizza or grabbing something quick, but instinct tugged him toward the kitchen instead. He opened the fridge more from habit than expectation—and was surprised to find a few groceries neatly arranged inside. On the top shelf, wrapped and waiting, sat a chicken sandwich with a small note attached:

I thought you'd be hungry, so I made you a bite.

A faint smile tugged at his lips. Probably the cleaning lady. Thoughtful.

He ate quietly at the kitchen counter, accompanied only by the hum of the refrigerator and the old house's soft creaks. For a moment, he could almost hear his grandparents' familiar chatter—his grandmother nudging his grandfather to take his medication, his grandfather groaning dramatically in protest. The memory brought a smile to Derek's face. He missed that.

Carrying his plate to the sink, he wandered into the living room. Each step deeper into the house felt like stepping into a museum curated from pieces of his childhood. Memories stirred with every glance.

He reached his grandparents' bedroom and paused in the doorway, staring at the neatly made bed. In his mind, he could still see them resting there—his grandfather's deep laugh, his grandmother's gentle smile. As a boy, he used to tiptoe in on weekend mornings and crawl between them, full of energy and ready to start the day. They never minded. They welcomed it.

Eventually, he turned and headed to the guest room—his room, really. Nothing had changed. The posters on the wall, the books on the shelves, the model cars lined up just as he'd left them. Even his old army photo sat on the nightstand in the same simple wooden frame.

He remembered coming home on leave—exhausted from long days on the road—only to be jolted awake by his grandfather's booming voice, eager to spend time with him. Downstairs, his grandmother would already be at the stove, the smell of blueberry pancakes filling the kitchen.

He could see it now—his grandmother standing over the skillet, his grandfather perched on a stool drinking coffee. His grandfather would turn toward him, eyes fixed lovingly on his wife, and say, "Did you ever see such a beautiful sight as this? I swear, your grandmother gets more lovely every day."

Derek would smile and agree.

And without fail, his grandmother would glance back and say with a laugh, "You both need glasses."

He lingered in that warmth for a moment. Then his thoughts shifted.

His relationship with Nancy had never been anything like what his grandparents shared. They had little in common. Even her friends were not the kind he would have chosen. If he were honest, Derek had always been a bit of a loner. But one thing was becoming clear—if he ever hoped to have a relationship worth holding onto, it would need to resemble the love his grandparents had. But was that even possible today?

For a time, he had believed his parents were in love, too. But his father's work kept him away most of the time. And when he was home, he was glued to the phone, his mind elsewhere. Derek had found more presence and stability with his grandparents. That was the kind of relationship he admired.

Not long before Derek joined the military, his grandfather had sat him down for one of those talks that seemed ordinary at the time but lingered for years afterward. Derek hadn't realized how relevant those words would become. Now, standing in the quiet of this house, he saw their weight.

His grandfather had warned him how easy it was to get tangled in the world's game. Whether you were a soldier, an important executive like his father, or simply trying to put food on the table—everyone wanted more for themselves and their children. But that hunger, if left unchecked, was the same seed sown in the Garden. Adam and Eve believed the Lie—that God was withholding something—and ever since, people have been grasping for more, often at the cost of what matters most.

Derek thought of his father, who had finally realized that life was more than chasing after something. Life began with faith—and continued on a journey of faith.

Derek exhaled deeply. He was tired. The day had been long. His encounter with Althea, his talk with Great-grandfather Roberts, his time at the bridge—all of it pressed on his mind. It was time to rest.

He crawled into bed, wondering what tomorrow might bring.

The Dream.

It wasn't long after Derek's head touched the pillow that he was taken somewhere—transported beyond the borders of sleep.

The wind stirred on the Hill where he stood overlooking Jerusalem. The city rested beneath a darkened sky, quiet yet heavy, as though warned of a coming storm. The air itself seemed thick enough to taste, pressing against Derek's chest with the weight of an unseen dread, as if something terrible was moments away.

From the shadows beside him, an old man stepped forward. His robe was weathered and torn, carrying the dust and history of ages. A leather belt cinched his waist, and in his hand he held a wooden staff smoothed by years of use. His beard was white as snow, and his eyes burned like coals—sharp, fierce, yet alive with an unshakable hope. When he spoke, his voice rolled across the hills like distant thunder.

"Jerusalem will become a cup of trembling to all the surrounding nations…"

Below them, Derek saw armies gathering—multitudes from many nations encircling the city. Their banners whipped in the wind; their faces were set in anger and determination. Fear tightened Derek's chest as the ground trembled beneath the weight of their advance. Zechariah's voice deepened as the vision intensified.

The earth quaked with the march of soldiers. The walls were breached. Smoke spiraled into the sky as cries filled the streets.

"The city will be taken," Zechariah continued, "the houses plundered, the women violated. Half of Jerusalem will go into captivity… but the remnant of the people shall not be cut off."

Amid the devastation, Derek saw them—the faithful

remnant. Their clothes were torn, their world collapsing around them, yet they stood unbowed. Their eyes were lifted upward, anchored in hope stronger than the ruins beneath their feet.

Zechariah turned to him, grief etched deeply across his face, but certainty shining just as strongly.

"Many claim the promises have passed from Israel to another," he said, "but hear the words of the Apostle Paul: Has God rejected His people? By no means! We are but wild branches grafted in, nourished by the root of God's covenant. The gifts and calling of God are irrevocable."

Derek's throat tightened.

Why does this feel so close? So personal? So many lives hanging in the balance…

Then, out of the corner of his eye, he noticed something— a quiet eagle standing near Israel. Calm. Peaceful. Loyal. The eagle watched the growing storm with gentle eyes, but its wings remained folded. It made only mild protests while the nations stirred in anger around Jerusalem.

Why is the eagle silent? Derek wondered. Is friendship enough when the storm breaks? Has the eagle grown weak? Is this what it means?

Before the question settled, the heavens split open.

Light brighter than the sun poured forth. A figure descended—robed in glory, crowned with majesty, His eyes blazing like fire. His voice roared like rushing waters. Upon His head were many crowns. His robe was dipped in blood. And written on His thigh:

KING OF KINGS AND LORD OF LORDS.

Derek's heart thundered. Tears blurred his vision as the Mount of Olives split beneath the Messiah's feet—living water bursting forth, flowing through the shattered city, bringing healing wherever it touched. The armies scattered like chaff before a raging wind.

He remembered Dirk's words: Christ Himself will intervene and save Israel.

Tears streamed down Derek's face—not only for the destruction he witnessed but for the overwhelming promise of redemption and victory. Zechariah's voice rose again, trembling with joy.

"On that day, the Lord will defend the inhabitants of Jerusalem; the city shall be called the Faithful City."

Is there hope for all of us? Derek wondered.

Zechariah's final words lingered in the air like an echo stretching beyond the vision:

"Yet many still walk blind, unaware of what draws near…"

Derek thought of the chaos unfolding in the world today. His grandfather's voice echoed through the vision: "Fear not, and do Christ's business."

Suddenly, the scene shifted.

Derek now stood in the midst of a great multitude. Around him, people moved mechanically in every direction. Their faces were hidden behind blank, lifeless masks—emotionless, expressionless. They walked in a dull, endless rhythm, unaware, untouched, unsmiling. No laughter. No tears. Only the slow march of souls who did not know they were asleep.

Then one figure caught his eye.

A woman—unmasked.

Her face was open and alive, her eyes cutting through the veil of indifference that blanketed the crowd. She looked directly at Derek, and only then did he realize he, too, wore a mask. His mask, like the others, had no eyes. They all spoke, but none of them seemed aware of what they were saying.

The woman's unmasked gaze searched him deeply, reaching past the surface—seeing into his very soul.

Who is she? he wondered. Is she the hope I'm searching for? Or is she the warning?

"The King is coming!" she cried, her voice ringing like a clear trumpet blast.

But the crowd did not turn. They continued drifting aimlessly, oblivious and unmoved. Though aware of the chaos swirling around them, their eyes still clung to false hopes. Leaders lifted their hands, pointing in every direction.

"The problem is there—to the east!"

"No, to the north—guard yourselves against him!"

Finger by finger, voice by voice, blame was cast—yet no one looked within. They built bigger weapons, stronger walls, louder threats—but still no peace. The air trembled with their striving, and their hands—empty and shaking—reached out for something real. Reached out for hope. But found none.

A deep sorrow gripped Derek's heart. How many were walking blindly through life, missing what mattered most? The weight of their blindness pressed upon him like a stone.

He opened his mouth to speak—

but the scene dissolved.

Derek awoke, heart pounding, eyes wet with tears. Haunted yet hopeful. Burdened and stirred to watch and wait for that Day.

His grandfather's voice echoed in his memory—the Day when Christ Himself would appear, when the King would return in glory. Then the Scripture his grandfather often quoted seemed to rise before him. His lips trembled as he whispered into the darkness, clinging to the words he remembered:

"For the Lord Himself will descend from heaven with a cry of command… and we will be caught up… to meet the Lord in the air. The voice of an archangel, and the sound of the trumpet of God."

Derek sat up slowly, his mind swirling with images and questions. The weight of the vision pressed on his heart, uncertainty gnawing at him. Then one thought struck with piercing clarity:

I wore a mask too… What am I blind to? Am I any different from them?

The question lingered—heavy, unshakable—as though the dream had only just begun its work in him.

What was he to do with such a dream?

Then another memory surfaced—his grandfather's worn journal, filled with stories and wisdom. Derek remembered reading how, after every powerful encounter, his grandfather would seek counsel from his closest friend, Greg, a man who helped him make sense of dreams and visions.

"No vision is meant to be carried alone," his grandfather had once written, almost like a quiet confession to himself.

Those words—no vision meant to be carried alone—pressed on Derek now, mingling with the echoes of his own dream: the mask, the crowd, the woman's piercing eyes.

That's what I need to do, he thought, a sense of urgency tightening in his chest. Yes… that is what I need to do.

Determined, he rose and whispered to himself,

"I'm going to see Uncle Greg."

Chapter 6

When The Heart Makes Room

"Even in a world that runs without pause, the soul cannot thrive without stillness before its Creator. When we choose to dwell with Christ, His presence reshapes us in ways we could not never have imagined. – Reflection.

"Be still, and know that I am God; I will be exalted among the nations, I will be exalted in the earth." -- Psalm 46:10

Derek rose from bed, still carrying the weight of the night pressing against his chest. The images from Zechariah's prophecy—the masked crowd, the woman without a mask, her piercing warning—lingered like shadows on the walls of his mind. The unease hadn't faded, yet beneath it was a quiet pull urging him toward something deeper.

He set a fresh cup of coffee beside him and reached for his grandfather's journal. The worn leather felt familiar, like the hand of a friend who always knew how to listen. Flipping through its pages, he stopped at the familiar slanted script:

"Moses went up the mountain to be with God for forty days, and when he came down, he was changed. His face shone so brightly the people could not look at him. Scripture tells us of this physical change so we might understand the deeper truth: you cannot spend that much time with God and remain the same inside. I know it is difficult in our fast-paced world to find time, but even the smallest choice to acknowledge Him can open the door for change. When you wake, simply open your eyes and say, Good morning, Jesus. On your way to work, talk to Him. Tell Him you want Him to be part of your day, that you want to be aware of Him and the opportunities He has prepared for you. Do this constantly, and you will see a change that no one can take away."

Derek leaned back as the words settled into him. Somehow, in the middle of his restless thoughts, his grandfather's voice rose like still water—reminding him that even the busiest heart can make room for Christ.

On the side table lay his grandfather's Bible, opened to Luke 10:41–42, the words underlined:

"Martha, Martha," the Lord answered, "you are worried and upset about many things, but few things are needed—or indeed only one. Mary has chosen what is better, and it will not be taken away from her."

In the margin, his grandfather had written, see Psalm 46:10:

"Be still, and know that I am God;

I will be exalted among the nations,

I will be exalted in the earth."

Derek closed his eyes, journal resting in his hands, letting the words settle in his spirit. Moses spent time with God—but even a simple Good morning, Jesus could shift the direction of a day. Talk to Him. Invite Him into your day. You will see your life change.

He shut the journal and leaned back with a thoughtful sigh.

The sudden ringing of his phone startled him.

Nancy.

A strange discomfort stirred—not because he didn't want to talk to her, but because something in him hesitated. Still, he answered.

"Good morning, Nancy."

"I was expecting your call," she said.

"I know I should have called," Derek replied, "but so much has happened. I saw my great-grandfather… being in his presence was like being with Jesus."

Nancy's tone sharpened. "You're not on that Jesus thing

again, are you?"

"I just know I need more than I have," Derek said—sharper than he intended. He softened his voice. "Nancy, I told you about my family… how they had something special. I need that in my life."

She brushed past his words. "Some of the Western leaders are arriving in Washington today, and I'm covering the story. They're talking about BRICS, and President Trump isn't happy the world is pivoting away from the U.S. dollar. America's influence is slipping. Leaders from the UK, France, Germany, and Canada are calling for more global unity. They're saying the world needs less religion. And they want Trump to back away from Israel."

Her last words made Derek stiffen.

The dream.

Zechariah.

The nations gathered.

Jerusalem—a cup of trembling.

"Derek, are you still there?" Nancy asked.

"Yes… I'm listening."

She continued, "Israel is causing too many problems. They think they're God's chosen people. Religion only creates conflict. Imagine if there were none. Like John Lennon's song— Imagine… no Heaven, no religion. It really is easy to imagine. And honestly? I agree with him."

There was a brief pause on the line before Nancy spoke again, her tone softer than before.

"I suppose you see things differently."

"Yes," Derek replied firmly. "Just because Christianity has had a spotted history doesn't make it wrong—no more than something good becoming twisted makes the thing itself evil. People can take something beautiful and use it for destruction. That doesn't mean the beauty was never real. Think of medicine. It can heal, save lives, and bring hope. But in the wrong hands, the same substance can poison and kill. The problem isn't the medicine; it's how it's used."

Silence followed, and when Nancy spoke again, her voice carried a reluctant gentleness.

"I suppose… you make a good point."

"When are you coming back?" she asked.

"I'm not sure," Derek said. "There's a lot I need to do."

"Don't forget about me," she said quietly. "I've got to get to work—it's a busy day."

They said their goodbyes, and Derek hung up. But the uneasiness inside him didn't fade.

He sat in the quiet after the call, the silence almost pressing against him. Nancy's words had carried more than disagreement—they revealed the widening gap between the path she chose and the one stirring in his own heart. Two worlds pulling at him, like the water below and the sky above when he had stood on the bridge the night before.

One path spoke loudly—fast, crowded, full of voices telling him what to think and what to believe.

The other felt quieter, mysterious, like a road half-hidden in fog… yet alive—pulling him in with a gravity he could no longer deny.

He thought again of his grandfather's wisdom: Find time to be with God, and your life will change in ways you cannot imagine.

And as the memory of his dream returned—nations in turmoil, people drifting blindly, and the lone woman crying out— he felt certain the two were connected, whispering of change he could no longer ignore.

After his reflection, Derek rose from his chair, the weight of Nancy's words still hanging in the air. He walked to the garage. The door creaked open, revealing his grandfather's Harley-Davidson—an early 2000s model, sleek, black, and gleaming under the dim light as if it had just left the showroom.

Though his grandfather rode it less in his later years, he never parted with it. Derek could almost hear his voice again, saying he felt God's presence every time the engine rumbled beneath him. Beside the bike sat an old leather easy chair, worn in all the right places. When he could no longer ride, his grandfather would sit there for hours, gazing at the Harley as though it were a window into another world.

Derek smiled at the memory. As a boy he used to ask his grandmother where Grandfather was. She would nod toward the garage with a knowing smile.

"Out riding his bike," she'd say—and then whisper, "spending time with Jesus."

Leaning against the workbench, Derek's thoughts drifted to a story from the journal—one of his grandfather's most powerful memories.

His grandfather had visited Pastor Roberts for counsel. During prayer, he felt a tug deep in his spirit—a nudge toward someone who used to attend the church but had long fallen out of contact. The impression was simple: Go to 3rd Street. Number three. He didn't know why. He simply obeyed.

He had pulled into the driveway of a small, weatherworn house, pretending his motorcycle was having trouble so he could ask to use the phone. As he walked toward the door, he prayed silently for God to guide his steps.

Then he saw her.

The woman in the front window.

His woman—the same woman from his dream. Her eyes were wide, silently pleading for help. She was being held captive by her mentally ill husband.

What happened next changed everything. His grandfather intervened. Help arrived. A life was spared.

And it was on the ride home—on that same Harley—that he saw Melissa for the first time. She was the other woman from his dream, standing in the window, longing to come in. It was there, with God's presence stirring in his heart, that he knelt down and asked her to marry him.

This bike wasn't just a machine—it was woven into the very fabric of their family's story.

The story from his grandfather's journal meant more to Derek than he realized. It stirred something deep—something long dormant. He wanted Jesus in his life in a more personal way. Not because his grandfather had been flawless. He hadn't been. He carried scars and shortcomings, just like Jacob, David, and Paul.

Jacob was a deceiver.

David, a man of deep faith, also knew profound failure.

Paul once refused to take Mark on his missionary journey, leading to a sharp disagreement with Barnabas.

Yet God used them all.

None of them were perfect; only One ever was—and is—Jesus.

God uses willing, flawed people.

Derek bowed his head and prayed a simple prayer.

Jesus, I may never have encounters with You like my grandfather did—and that's okay. I do, however, need You in my life. For too long I've been drifting. I still don't know where my next steps will take me, but I want the simple faith I had as a child. I may never be a champion of faith like others, but I want to be Yours. I want a true relationship with You. Forgive me. I was blind. Teach me.

He sat quietly for a long moment, letting the words settle. Slowly, the weight in his chest loosened. The meaning of all this was still unclear—yet he knew one thing: something in his life had shifted. Something was turning.

His gaze drifted to his grandfather's motorcycle.

"I guess you're mine now," he said softly.

Without overthinking it, he knew where he needed to go. Uncle Greg might have answers—or at least the kind of listening ear his grandfather always trusted… the kind that carried no judgment and no pressure.

The decision came simply. Derek grabbed his helmet, kicked the stand up, and fired the engine to life. The road to Greg's place wasn't far, and Derek hoped the ride itself would help him sort through everything God was stirring in his heart.

The familiar thrum vibrated through the frame. It had been a while since he had ridden, yet the motion felt like slipping into an old memory. He eased out of the driveway, the mid-morning cool brushing his face, wind needling his eyes as the road stretched out before him.

"Teach me," he whispered into the rushing air.

The ride steadied him.

The scent of freshly mowed grass.

Storefronts sliding past.

A dog barking behind a familiar fence.

And then Uncle Greg's house came into view.

Derek pulled into the driveway and cut the engine.

The sudden quiet rang in his ears.

Uncle Greg's.

The screen door creaked as Greg stepped outside. "I'd know that sound anywhere," he said with a grin. "Takes me back to all those times your grandfather's bike sat out there."

They embraced warmly.

"It's so good to see you," Greg said.

"I meant to answer those letters," Derek admitted, "but… you know."

"That's fine," Greg replied. "You're here now—that's what matters. You didn't let anyone know you were coming, just like your grandfather."

"Only been a couple of days," Derek said. "I visited Great-Grandfather Roberts first."

They started walking toward the house. Inside, Aunt Diane greeted him with a hug and a smile.

"Well, look who finally decided to show up," Diane teased warmly.

Greg chuckled. "We were just talking about your grandfather, Dirk."

Derek smiled faintly. "I suppose I'm trying to follow his tire tracks in some ways."

Greg realized, as Derek said it, that he had come carrying something heavy on his mind.

"Derek," Greg said, looking at him directly, "you look like a man on a mission… or chased by a dream."

"Two dreams," Derek answered. "And a phone call that wouldn't let me catch my breath."

Diane gestured toward a warm, cozy room. "You men can talk here while I prepare lunch for us."

She left, and Greg and Derek settled into what was about to become a serious conversation. Greg leaned forward, his voice quiet but edged with curiosity.

"You said something about dreams and a phone conversation."

Derek took a slow breath. "Both dreams feel connected. Mine was about Zechariah 12–14 and Revelation 12. Grandfather Dirk's dream was about the four horsemen. Together, they gave a startling picture." He turned his grandfather's worn journal in his hands. "He also wrote about a dream in which an angel blew a trumpet, and in the margin he pinned Revelation 14:7."

Greg, looking shaken, said, "The pastor spoke about the judgment of the trumpets last Sunday." He opened his Bible and read aloud, " 'Fear God and give Him glory, because the hour of His judgment has come. Worship Him who made the heavens, the earth, the sea, and the springs of water.' "

Derek tapped the note his grandfather had left: "In the last days, old men will dream dreams and young men will see visions." (Joel 2:28). "I remember Pastor Roberts telling me that some people see that verse fulfilled at Pentecost… but he said biblical prophecy can often have a double meaning—true then, and still pointing to a future fulfillment."

Greg nodded. "That's exactly what the pastor said last Sunday. It reminds me of a conversation your grandfather and I once had. It's not new, but it puts yours in context. Ever since your grandfather's dream, there's been a growing interest in prophecy—people waking up to the idea that these aren't just stories. They carry guidance for our times."

As Greg spoke, Derek's mind drifted back to his dream—masked crowds pressing forward, the city trembling, voices swallowed by chaos. He leaned back thoughtfully.

Greg continued, "Your grandfather, Dirk, used to say that the West has taken God's blessing for granted—and worse, that they no longer see their blessings as a gift from Him. He was right. We read the Bible and think, nice stories, as if they have nothing to do with us. But they have everything to do with us. We either learn from history or live to experience its consequences."

He paused, then added more quietly, "Your dream reveals what's happening now: the West is losing its global influence. It's tried to control things for decades. BRICS will succeed, and no matter how hard America or the West try to stop it, they won't—because we've taken advantage. We've drifted from God."

God chose a people to bear His message to the world. They failed again and again, and we see the consequences. Yet God hasn't given up on Israel, even though most haven't recognized Jesus as Messiah. "Your dream, Derek, about Zechariah," Greg continued, "says nations will turn against Israel—we can see that rising now. Anti-Semitism is growing globally. But Zechariah also tells how Christ Himself will save the Jewish people."

Derek's mind slipped back into the dream: armies tightening around Jerusalem, the city shaking, half ravaged yet a remnant unbroken; the Lamb standing. He remembered the line that had rung in his chest: "On that day, the Lord will defend the inhabitants of Jerusalem; the city shall be called the faithful city."

Greg's voice drew him back. "Your dreams are more than visions; they're a call. To pray. To be alert. To spread the message and walk in truth. That's the difference between wandering and following."

Greg paused, studying Derek's face. "And the second dream—the one with the multitude and the masks?"

Derek nodded, voice low. "I stood among a crowd—everyone wearing masks, and their masks had no eyes. Empty, emotionless faces moving mechanically. Then I saw her, one woman without a mask. She looked straight at me… and I had on a mask."

"And what did you feel?" Greg asked gently.

"Like she could see through me, past everything I was hiding. She cried out, 'The King is coming,' and no one noticed. I felt sorrow for so many walking blindly, missing what matters most."

Greg's voice drew him back again. "Your dreams are more than visions; they're a call to pray, to be alert, to spread the message, and to walk in truth. That's the difference between wandering and following."

The conversation paused as Diane entered the room, smiling. "Lunch is ready." The seriousness of the discussion eased as they moved toward the kitchen, and the talk shifted to more ordinary topics—gardens, the weather, and old neighbors.

As they ate, Diane suddenly said, "I wish Jennifer were here—she would love to see you."

Derek smiled faintly. "I remember Jennifer from our school days. Feels like ages ago."

Greg chuckled. "She still talks about those days."

"Where is she?" Derek asked.

Greg and Diane looked at their watches and answered together, as if rehearsed: "She's gone to her Hill."

The phrase caught Derek's attention. He'd heard it so often when he was younger, and he had just gone looking for it a day ago. He didn't press for more, but the thought lingered in his mind.

Derek's eyes wandered around the room, landing on a

framed picture of a young woman wearing a stethoscope and a white coat, her smile bright and steady. He leaned forward. "I remember… you had another daughter, too, didn't you? Jenny?"

A gentle silence fell. Diane's gaze softened. "Yes. Jenny was our firstborn. Strong-willed, compassionate—always running ahead, wanting to help someone."

"I think I remember her. I was so young," Derek said.

"She was a lot like her aunt Jenny, the one she was named after," Diane added softly.

Derek leaned forward. "I read about Aunt Jenny in Grandfather's journal. She died of cancer, yet God allowed her to come back and guide Grandfather for a time."

Diane nodded gently. "That's right. We named our daughter after Greg's sister, Jenny. She became a doctor in the Congo, and whenever she came home, she would tell us about the miracles God was doing there. But one day, she gave her life in the service of protecting others who believed in Jesus."

Derek's eyes widened. "She died because of believing in Jesus? You hear about things, but they don't really hit you until they hit home."

Greg nodded. "Yes. Our country hasn't reached that point

yet, but Christian freedoms in the West are slowly eroding. In Canada, a teacher cannot hold Christian values if they do not align with LGBTQ policies. In the UK, it is unlawful to pray in public in certain places."

Derek hesitated. "Excuse me, I don't want to be rude, but I don't understand—there were miracles, but no miracle to save your daughter?"

Diane spoke with a tender but firm voice. "It isn't easy to understand. But this is an upside-down world full of evil, as your Aunt Jenny, the one who died of cancer, used to say. And I heard your grandmother, Melissa, say it as well: 'We don't always understand what God is doing, but we can always trust Him.' He doesn't just want our trust when life is easy; he also wants it when life makes no sense. Perhaps you remember what Jesus said to Thomas: 'Because you have seen me, you have believed; blessed are those who have not seen and yet have believed.' This is the same when life becomes difficult."

Greg nodded slowly. "We still grieve, but we also trust in a God who is bigger than our grief. Years later, when we thought our time for raising children was long past, God gave us another daughter. We named her Jennifer—and that name is a reminder to us of God's gift. A blessing. She has grown now, walking her own path, and has her own Hill. You two may have more history than you realize."

The phrase gone to her Hill echoed in Derek's mind. Now he understood. Jenny's Hill had been a sacrifice; Jennifer's—and his—Hill was still ahead, waiting to be climbed.

There was a quiet pause. Greg asked Derek about his plans.

"Have you considered moving back home?"

Derek shook his head. "My path right now seems clouded."

"Your path will become clearer," Diane said gently.

After a while, Derek pushed his chair back. "I should be going."

"Already?" Greg asked.

"It was great being here, but I must be going," Derek said.

Greg hesitated, then said gently, "Before you go, may I pray with you?"

Derek nodded.

Greg bowed his head. "Lord Jesus, thank You for bringing Derek here today. I sense he is searching, though his Hill is not yet clear. Show him, Lord, the Hill You have chosen for him, and make his path straight. Let him know You walk with him, just as You've walked with us. In Your name, Amen."

Diane spoke softly, "Amen."

They walked him to the door. Diane embraced Derek. "Thanks for coming. Hope to see you again."

"Me too," Derek replied.

He stepped out, the late afternoon sun spilling across the sky. Mounting his bike, he glanced back once more before heading down the lane toward home; gone to her Hill echoed in his thoughts.

The hum of the motorcycle filled the quiet country road, but in Derek's mind, the echoes of the day were louder than any engine. Zechariah's visions, the Four Horsemen, the angel with the trumpet—they all pressed on him with a weight he couldn't shake. Perhaps most of all, Jennifer…gone to her Hill. The phrase repeated like a heartbeat, a reminder that life was moving forward, that purpose awaited, even if he didn't yet see it clearly.

He slowed the bike near a bend in the road, the late afternoon sun casting long shadows across the fields. For the first time in weeks, he allowed himself to breathe—not just the air around him, but deeply, letting his thoughts settle.

He thought of the woman in his second dream—the one without a mask. Her eyes had seen him in a way no one else had. And in the quiet after the phone call with Nancy, he realized what he truly longed for: a relationship with Jesus, simple, personal, real. Not perfection. Not accolades. Just guidance, presence, and truth.

By the time he reached his driveway, the sky was streaked with amber and violet. He opened the garage door, drove in, and cut the engine. Sitting there for a moment, helmet in his hand, Derek whispered a prayer he hadn't said aloud:

"Jesus, I don't have many answers. I may never have the encounters Grandfather did. But I need You. I want to follow You, not just know about You. Teach me. Be with me. Let my life reflect You, even in small ways. I choose You. I pray this in Your name—Jesus."

Derek felt unsettled; the road ahead still seemed confusing, and he was unsure of his next steps.

Chapter 7

Two Paths

"Life often presents us with choices between the familiar and the faithful. The path of ease may feel safe, but it rarely leads to growth or purpose." -- Reflection.

"Trust in the Lord with all your heart and lean not on your own understanding; in all your ways submit to Him, and He will make your paths straight." -- Proverbs 3:5-6.

Derek lay in bed and looked around at all the memorabilia in the room. Life had been so much simpler back then. His boyhood had indeed been a happy one. Yet, as he reflected, he realized that many young people today have never known that simpler life. Many parents now struggle just to get by, and in some cities, homelessness is a growing problem. The darkness in the world is not fading but spreading, though we are told to believe it has always been this way. Once, such troubles seemed distant—flashes on a television screen in faraway countries; few paid attention. But now, it is worldwide. And still, leaders talk of more military arms, faster weapons to kill. His grandfather, Dirk, had written that the Bible says the world will grow more conflicted, and more trouble will continue as time goes on, for the evil one knows his time is short.

As Derek lay there, his mind circled the words of his uncle's prayer. *"Show him his Hill and make his path straight."* The words echoed until sleep finally claimed him.

And that was when the dream came.

Derek stood on a narrow ridge between two valleys. At first, they seemed simple: one smooth and well-worn, almost inviting; the other rougher, twisting into uncertainty. But as he looked closer, both paths split into many, each branching into countless choices. Each road divided endlessly before him until they wove together like a web, forming two paths.

To his right, a wide road stretched out, filled with crowds of people laughing, singing, and carrying on as though life had no end. Bright lights flashed, music pounded, and the street seemed alive with celebration. Yet, the further Derek looked, the darker the path became, until it disappeared into a shadow he could not see beyond.

To his left, another road began. This one was narrower, with only a few people walking on it. Some stumbled, some wept, some pressed forward with tired steps. There were many hills to climb. His mind wandered to the old story of Pilgrim's Progress by John Bunyan. The image in Bunyan's story was of the pilgrim pressing toward the Celestial City, which rose in his thoughts. Yet this felt different. Bunyan's journey was about finding salvation, but Derek already believed he was saved. The question for him now was different: what does he do after returning to Christ? The road ahead seemed much more challenging, with obstacles at every turn. Nancy came to mind, along with friends who would not understand his change. The path looked costly if he was to be more than a fence-walker.

Every turn carried the weight of choice—not just for him but for the world. It was as though every step forward multiplied the decisions before him, and there was no clear end in sight. Every step was more than a decision—it was an allegiance.

From behind came the voices of the past: words of encouragement tangled with accusations, love entwined with bitterness, the ache of family turned distant. They were reminders that choices never ended with the one who made them—they rippled outward across generations.

At the center of it all stood a man with a mask. But it was more than a mask—the mask had no eyes and no mouth. The man trembled, caught between these paths. A woman's voice urged, "Remove the mask." The air thickened with conflict, for the mask was more than a disguise; it was a denial, a refusal to face what was true. Nearby, an angel waited—sword drawn, light blazing against the shadows that crept across the paths. The angel did not force the man forward but stood as a reminder: the divine was present even amid chaos. Every choice mattered. Every step was a stand in the battle between God's way and the pull of evil.

Derek woke with a heavy sense of restlessness, the images from his dream still pressing against his mind. His chest felt tight as he wrestled with his thoughts—Nancy's choice, his own life, and what he truly wanted. Diane's words from the visit echoed in his head.

What are your plans?

All of it seemed to converge, yet the meaning of the mask in his dream remained elusive. After a shower, he sat at the kitchen counter, sipping a cup of coffee, wondering what he was going to do today. He considered calling Nancy, but what could he say? He knew she wanted answers, but he still didn't have any. That must be the reason for the dream. He felt as though everything was pulling at him, and the man in his dream was uncertain about which path to take.

Derek's thoughts turned to his great-grandfather, Roberts. Perhaps he could help explain the dream. He dressed and returned to the kitchen counter, coffee in hand. He knew he needed to call Nancy—she would be expecting it—but what could he say? The only decision he had truly settled was that he needed Christ in his life. Beyond that, everything else felt like his dream: he was stuck, unsure of his next direction.

Reaching for the phone, a knock came at the door. Derek hesitated, then opened it.

An attractive brunette stood there, smiling. "You're not going to invite me in?" she asked.

Derek blinked, surprise written across his face.

"You don't remember me, do you?" she blurted.

He looked closer, and then recognition struck. "Jennifer…" he whispered, pulling her into a sudden, tight embrace.

"You can let go anytime now," she chuckled.

They stepped inside. Derek motioned toward the counter. "Coffee?" he offered.

"One sugar, one cream," she answered without hesitation. Jennifer cradled her mug, letting the steam rise between them.

"So, Derek…how are you really doing?"

He leaned back against the counter, staring into the dark swirl of his coffee. "Honestly? I was drawn home to try to make sense of my life. What I've come to realize so far is this—I need Jesus. But beyond that, my life is no clearer. Everything else feels like my dream. I'm stuck, and I don't know where to go next."

Jennifer nodded slowly. "It sounds like you need a change."

Derek looked at her with a half-smile. "What about you? What's your life been like?"

She sighed, twirling the spoon in her cup. "My life was…complicated. I got off track. Did some things I'm not proud of."

Derek raised an eyebrow. "You? Get in trouble? You were the one the family thought had everything together."

"That," she said softly, "was part of the problem. I had a dead Aunt Jenny who walked with God—Dad's sister. She helped guide your grandfather, Dirk, to the bridge where he met your grandmother, Melissa. And then my sister, Jenny—who was named after Aunt Jenny—died on the mission field, giving her life for Christ. How do you live up to that kind of legacy? They even named me Jennifer." She paused. "I couldn't. I pushed against it, did some foolish things, but Pastor Roberts helped put my feet on solid ground and made me see I didn't need to live to that legacy. God can use each of us in different ways. Now I'm living for Christ."

Derek studied her for a moment, then gave a small nod. "I guess everyone has their struggles."

Jennifer smiled. "Yes, and we tend to think ours are the worst—but they're just different."

Derek asked, "I suppose you have somebody in your life?"

Jennifer smiled again. "I do, but if you mean a man, no—I do not. I am past that. That's one thing I did learn from my Aunt Jenny's legacy."

Both of them spoke at once, grinning as their words overlapped.

"Anything worth having is worth waiting for." And *"we must know the difference between feelings and truth."* They chuckled.

"We heard that a hundred times when we were teenagers," Dirk said.

"More like a thousand," Jennifer smiled, lifting her mug.

Jennifer leaned back, her eyes softening. "That brings me to the reason I came this morning. Derek, I know you have your teaching credentials. There's a Grade 10 history position open at our school—the very one we both attended. I remember you majored in history and always loved it."

Derek looked intrigued. "Who would I even talk to about something like that?"

Jennifer smiled. "Me."

Derek blinked, puzzled. "You?"

"I'm the principal at the high school," she said, almost playfully. "If I submitted your name, the board would accept it without question."

Derek sat back, shaking his head slowly. "You're the principal? And here I thought you were still figuring life out. Looks like you've got it together."

She laughed lightly. "Eventually, yes, but that doesn't mean I have everything figured out. There is a catch—or rather, two."

"What are the two?" Derek asked, wary.

"First, I'd be your boss," she said matter-of-factly. "And second, you'd need to take a two-week refresher course. It starts in three weeks. All new teachers from outside the district have to take it."

Derek frowned, uncertainty written across his face. "But Jennifer, you don't really know anything about me."

She met his eyes without hesitation. "I know enough. You love teaching history. And you love Jesus. That's all I need to know—the rest will work itself out."

For a moment, Derek didn't know what to say.

Jennifer glanced at her watch and stood. "I must be going. But don't take too long to get back to me, Derek. I really do need to fill this position."

He rose with her, and they exchanged a gentle goodbye, remarking on how good it felt to see one another again. As she stepped through the door, she turned back one last time. "Go to your Hill. You'll find the answer there."

The door clicked shut, and silence settled over the room. Derek leaned against the table, his mind running faster than his heart could keep up. Work. Faith. Nancy. Friends. Now, this unexpected offer. More than ever, the road before him felt like a path filled with choices—uncertain, uphill, but unavoidable.

Yet, as he stood there, another thought lingered, one he couldn't quite push away. There had been something about Jennifer—something steady and sure in her presence—that stirred him. He had enjoyed being in her company more than he had expected. Perhaps it was his memories, but there was more; there was a mystery in it, as if her words carried weight beyond the conversation itself.

"Go to your Hill; you will find the answer," she had said before leaving. Derek repeated the words softly under his breath. The Hill, he knew, was more than a place—but he wasn't like his grandfather, who seemed to walk with God. He needed a bit more clarity.

But the Hill was always there in the distance—that was one reason he had come home to revisit his Hill. And we know how that turned out. It was gone. Was Jennifer speaking out of simple encouragement? Maybe he could have asked her about her Hill. Maybe he could have gone to her Hill. Could God be speaking through her words, pointing him back to the very place where life had been simpler? A time long gone. Derek felt the stirring of something larger than himself. The Hill was calling again.

Chapter 8

The Path Made Straight.

"There are times in life when the path before us seems twisted, lost among shadows and turns we cannot see beyond. Yet God does not ask us to clear the way ourselves—He promises to make the path straight when we trust Him—it does not mean an easy one." -- Reflection.

"I will go before you and make the crooked places straight; I will break in pieces the gates of bronze and cut the bars of iron." -- Isaiah 45:2

The morning light filtered through the window. Derek stood with his head bowed, shoulders heavy, then raised his eyes toward heaven.

"God, I've realized life can be twisted and uncertain. Full of turns. I don't understand. If I understand Jennifer correctly, 'You don't ask me to figure it all out alone.' You promise to make the crooked places straight when I trust You. That doesn't mean the road will be easy, but it will be sure. I suppose, God, that's what I read in Grandfather Dirk's journal: the path may not always be clear, but I can always trust You. If I follow the path You lead, I will be where I need to be. Now, Jesus, show me the path."

Derek took a deep breath, feeling a small measure of peace settle over him. The day was new, and perhaps—just perhaps—so was the start of his own path made straight.

He picked up the phone, knowing he should call Nancy, but his chest tightened. The conversation wouldn't be easy. He hadn't decided yet about the teaching position—and he wasn't even sure if he should mention it until he knew for certain. Some things could only be said in person.

Nancy answered on the second ring.

"Derek! I was wondering if you were going to call. When are you coming home?"

"Not sure," he replied cautiously. "It shouldn't be long."

"Great," she said, a note of relief in her voice. "When you get here, we need to start living. Don't bring up the marriage thing, but I've considered it…maybe in a couple of years. Oh! I have some great news." Her voice brightened. "I got that promotion! I'm now the senior White House reporter."

"That's great, Nancy. I'm so happy for you," Derek replied. "That's great for us—we can finally get a house."

Choosing his words carefully, Derek said, "We're going to need to talk when I get back."

"That sounds heavy," Nancy said, a little tension creeping into her voice.

"It's important," Derek replied quietly. "I have to go. I'm running late."

"Get home soon," she said hurriedly.

"I will. See you soon," Derek said, hanging up.

He set the phone down, heart still racing. Immediately, he thought there was no way they could live together. That much he knew. The path seemed complicated. What am I going to do?

No sooner had the words left his lips than his great-grandfather Roberts came to mind, with a strong, insistent pull he couldn't ignore. It was as if something deep in his heart was telling him he needed to see him—not just for guidance, but for clarity. He wondered whether Jennifer would go with him.

He picked up the phone again and called Jennifer.

"Hello?" she answered cheerfully.

Somewhat nervously, Derek asked, "Jennifer, would you…would you like to come with me to see great-grandfather Roberts?" He tried to sound casual.

There was a brief pause, then she laughed softly. "Yes! I was even thinking about doing that myself. I would love to."

"Great!" Derek said, relief flooding him. "When can I pick you up?"

"After lunch," Jennifer replied.

Derek's heart seemed at ease knowing she was going with him. He wasn't sure why, but he wanted her company. A sense of purpose built in him, knowing he had a companion along the way.

After lunch, Derek drove across town, pulling up in front of Uncle Greg's place. He had called earlier, assuming Jennifer still lived with her parents, but when he knocked, Uncle Greg chuckled and gave him the correct address. Shaking his head at himself, Derek climbed back into the car and drove on.

When he finally pulled up at Jennifer's place, she was already outside waiting. Her smile carried the same warmth that had steadied him the morning before when she knocked on his door. Sliding into the passenger seat, she glanced at him with a teasing grin.

"So you went to my parents' house first?"

Derek laughed a little sheepishly. "I did. Guess I thought you still lived there."

She shook her head, still smiling. "I love my parents very much, but I needed my own place. It was time."

The lightness of her voice eased him, and as they pulled away, he asked if she would mind if they took the Harley for the day.

Jennifer's eyes lit up. "Are you kidding? I'd love to."

Derek grinned. "I thought you might be interested, but I didn't want to assume. We can scoot back for it."

Jennifer's laughter warmed the car, and the ease between them grew. After a moment, Derek spoke again, his tone more thoughtful.

"Jennifer, yesterday you mentioned the Hill. I've been thinking about that ever since. What does the Hill mean to you?"

She turned toward the window for a moment, then back at him. "The Hill… it's more than just a place. For me, it's where I lay my burdens. It's where I can hear clearly—where all the clutter of life becomes quieted, and I can see both who I really am and who God is calling me to be."

Her words stirred something deep within Derek, mingling with the fragments of his dream. He tightened his grip on the wheel, nodding slowly. "I'm not even sure if I have a Hill, a special place. I talk to God, but it's not a place I go—like I did when I was a kid. I even took Grandfather Dirk there once. He told me, 'If you listen closely, you'll hear God.' Grandfather started by looking up to the heavens and saying, 'I am here today, sharing my grandson Derek and yours, special place, Jesus.' Then we sat there in silence for a while, and after he asked me what I had heard, I told him that I had heard bees dancing from flower to flower, birds singing as if thanking God for the day, and squirrels chasing one another like they were playing. He nodded and said, 'You are hearing.'"

Jennifer smiled softly. "He was wise."

She fell quiet, but inside her heart whispered, *Derek, you don't realize it yet, but you've already found your Hill.* Still, she said nothing, knowing it was something he needed to discover for himself.

A short while later, they pulled into Derek's driveway, and he wheeled the Harley out from the garage. The chrome caught the sun as if it had been waiting for this very day. When the engine rumbled to life, Jennifer's smile widened. She climbed on behind him, her arms circling his waist.

The ride was quiet, the warm wind rushing past as the road opened before them. Derek felt the freedom his grandfather must have loved—the steady rhythm on the bike grounding him even as it lifted his thoughts higher. *Now I see what grandfather felt,* he thought. *It's not just the ride; it's the presence, the clarity.* And as Jennifer's arms held him steady, he felt strangely glad she was there, close behind him.

Jennifer leaned gently against Derek, her thoughts wandering. *I wonder if Derek will take the teaching position. It would be good to have another Christian teacher by my side.* She paused, her cheek resting lightly on his shoulder. *And there's something steady, something different. Being near him makes me feel warm, safe, and even hopeful. That's not something I feel often, especially with men.*

Senior Living home.

Derek and Jennifer arrived at the senior living home in the early afternoon, the sun warm but mellow as it angled across the driveway. They walked through the entrance and approached the reception desk.

"Good day, madame. We are here to visit Pastor Roberts," Derek said politely.

The receptionist's eyes lit up.

"You must be his great-grandson, Derek, and his favorite niece, Jennifer."

Derek blinked, surprised.

"How did you know?"

The receptionist smiled warmly.

"Pastor Roberts told me to keep an eye out for you two. He is in his room, waiting."

As they walked toward the room, Derek leaned slightly toward Jennifer.

"You must have called him, letting him know we were coming."

Jennifer shook her head with a small smile.

"No, he just seems to know these things."

Pastor Roberts sat comfortably in his chair, a gentle light catching the edges of his back and silver hair. As they entered, he looked up, and his face brightened.

"Here are my favorite two young people," he said warmly. "Close the door behind you, grab those chairs, and pull up. I have been waiting for you."

Derek and Jennifer exchanged a quick smile before moving their chairs closer, anticipation and curiosity stirring in the air.

Jennifer leaned over and gave Pastor Roberts a gentle kiss on his cheek.

Pastor Roberts looked up, eyes softening.

"Lord, guide our conversation. May our words stir souls," he prayed quietly.

Then he turned his attention to Derek.

"Now, tell me about your new dream."

Derek raised his eyebrows, gathering his thoughts.

"Well… I see multitudes of people, all moving but seemingly going nowhere. They all wear masks. There is a web of paths, but all of them break down into two paths. They think it is the right path. When I look closer, I realize I am on that path too, but I have a mask with no eyes and no mouth."

Derek paused, then continued.

"Then there are two women. One is trying to pull me toward a path I know is wrong. The other woman has no mask. The woman without a mask is telling me to take off mine. I… I find it difficult to do."

Pastor Roberts nodded slowly, letting Derek's words settle.

"I see," he said quietly. "And how does it feel to be on that path, masked?"

Derek swallowed.

"It feels confusing. It feels lonely. I cannot see what is happening around me, so I cannot fully engage. I want to obey, to take off the mask, but it is hard. I am not sure yet."

Pastor Roberts studied Derek carefully.

"The mask in your dream represents darkness and blindness."

He leaned forward, turning his head to Jennifer and then back to Derek.

"The apostle Paul, in Colossians 1:16"—he flipped the pages to the verse—"says that all things were created through Him and for Him. Did you hear that? All things. That includes you, Jennifer, you, Derek, and me," he said as he pointed his finger.

"You and I were created for one reason only, to bring glory to Him. He created us. But that is when people clench their fists and cry, 'How dare you say such a thing. I am what is important. My desires, my choices.' That is the lie. Satan wants us to ask the wrong question: 'If there is a God, why do so many bad things happen?' That is not the question. The question is this: Why does this all-powerful God allow any of us to wake up in the morning? We believe the problem is out there somewhere. The problem is that the world is broken, and it is revealed in our hearts."

Pastor Roberts paused, letting the weight of his words settle.

"The forces of darkness want us to focus only on the evil that is out there. As long as we do, we can pretend we are not the problem. That explains your dream with people wearing masks. The apostle Paul says in verse 21 that in Christ, God put our feet on the right path. He made us right through the One for whom all things were created. So, the question you must answer is this: Are you going to live for the One you were created for, or for yourself?"

Derek's voice broke through the silence.

"I think I understand. I know Jesus died so I could be reconciled. But I still want a part of the world. I still want both. That is what I have been struggling with. It is my worldview."

Pastor Roberts looked at him with compassion.

"Yes, Derek. That is exactly it. And I will be honest with you, it took me a lifetime to learn this. I fought every step of the way. I fought even when I thought I was not fighting."

He leaned back thoughtfully.

"You may ask, 'What do you mean by that?' I mean this: your heart, my heart, are selfish. We resist Him by nature. But only when we take off the mask and face the truth can His light breathe through the darkness."

Pastor Roberts leaned forward. He looked Jennifer in the eyes, turned to Derek, and said,

"I know, I know, kids, and I say that with respect. To me, you are family. My words may sound like a sermon, but they are very important. I need you to understand this. I have little time left."

Jennifer and Derek spoke almost simultaneously.

"We want to hear what you say."

Then Derek added,

"Great-grandfather, your words bring clarity to my heart."

Pastor Roberts smiled, but with an earnest look on his face.

"We can get closer to God, but there is always that part of us that whispers, 'I am not as bad as that person.' There is a pull that says, 'I know better than His word.'"

He directed his question to both of them.

"Tell me, what man or woman, even if they are not sure about heaven or hell, does not assume they will make it into heaven? At least, if there is life beyond the grave, they believe they will be all right. That is blindness. That is the mask. The forces of darkness keep us looking outward, pointing fingers and measuring ourselves against others, rather than looking inward. The problem is not out there."

He placed his hand over his chest and tapped it firmly.

"The problem is right here. In this heart. In your mind. That is why Paul said to the Colossians, 'You were once alienated and enemies in your mind, yet now He has reconciled you.' Until we see that we have a mask on, you will always think you are fine, when in truth, you are blind."

Derek shifted in his seat, the words cutting closer than he expected.

Pastor Roberts reached out and gently tapped Derek on the shoulder. The touch was gentle, reassuring, but firm, as though urging Derek not to shrink back.

His voice softened.

"And do not look at me with some awe as if I am some holy man. I have struggled. I have fallen. My heart is sinful."

Jennifer's brows lifted slightly, surprised by what she was hearing.

"But Christ uses broken people who are willing to trust Him," Pastor Roberts continued. "Our sinful hearts tell us to give up when we fall, to hide in shame, or to justify our actions. Christ wants our hearts. That's where the battle is won."

He glanced between them, his gaze steady. "You need your sacred Hill. Go to Him there, again and again. That is where you will find strength."

Jennifer nodded faintly, her hand resting on her knee as though to steady herself. Derek kept his eyes on his great-grandfather, but something in him stirred—longing, and a little fear. Pastor Roberts turned his head and looked directly at Derek.

"Derek… in your dream, there were two women. Now, you tell me—what were they trying to do?"

Derek hesitated, then spoke slowly.

"One of them was pulling me, telling me things are okay and can get better, to keep to the road I am on, that the values of the Bible are archaic. That modern thinking, apart from God, is the path to walk." Derek swallowed, his brow furrowed. "But the other woman was different. She did not wear a mask, so she could see what others could not see. She wanted me to take off my mask and see what was happening. But it's more than that." Derek's voice grew stronger. "She was telling me not only to see but to speak. To take a stand."

Pastor Roberts nodded, eyes fixed on him. "Yes, Derek. That's it. What you just described is the struggle each of us faces. One voice tells you that God's old ways are outdated, unreal, and have no purpose. The other calls you to truth, to light, to Christ Himself. That pull is real because your heart is sinful, just like mine, just like everyone's. We all struggle; we all feel the tug toward the wrong path. God's Word guides us on the path to take."

Pastor Roberts paused, letting the words rest between them. Then he said, "Hear me—Christ calls the flawed. Jesus said, *'I come so that those who are blind will see, and those who think they see will be blind.'*"

His voice softened. "I know you know the path you need to take."

Jennifer's gaze lingered on Derek. In her heart, she wondered if she might be the woman from his dream—the one urging him to take off the mask and see. She prayed not only for him to take the teaching position but also to step into something greater: a true calling, a life in which his faith would shape more than just himself. Still, she said nothing. This had to be his decision.

Derek shifted slightly, sensing her eyes on him. He glanced her way, catching only the quiet steadiness in her expression. Whatever she was thinking, she kept it close, and he didn't press.

A soft knock tapped on the door.

Nurse Jody stepped in, holding a small cup of pills and a glass of water. Her eyes landed on Derek, and they lit up. "Nice to see you again, Derek."

Derek blinked in surprise. "You remembered me?"

Jody smiled. "Of course. Your great-grandfather talks about you often. And there"—she pointed to a picture hanging on the wall—"that's you with your grandparents."

Derek's eyes followed her finger, his expression softening as he saw the photo. There he was, younger, smiling between his grandparents, and he missed them. A warmth stirred in him, something he hadn't realized he had been longing for.

This… this is what I've been missing. A sense of family.

Turning back, Jody greeted warmly, "Hi, Jennifer, and thank you for the other night. I enjoyed it very much."

Jennifer gave a small smile and nodded. "Me too."

Jody then looked at Pastor Roberts with gentle firmness. "Grandfather, you need to take these pills."

Pastor Roberts accepted the cup, swallowed the medicine, and handed the container back to Jody with a sigh of contentment. His hand lifted slowly, pointing in a circle that encompassed them all. His voice carried the weight of love.

"You see what family really is? Derek and I are the only blood ties here, but being part of Christ's family makes us family." He smiled. "We are a family." He leaned back, then looked at Jody. "Do you work tomorrow?"

"Yes," she replied.

"Good." He shifted his gaze to Derek and Jennifer. "Could you both come tomorrow afternoon? And Jennifer, ask your parents to come as well."

The three of them exchanged surprised glances.

"What's up, Great-grandfather?" Derek finally asked.

Pastor Roberts only shook his head and smiled. "It's an important time. That's all I'll say."

Jennifer nodded softly. "We'll be here, and I'm sure Mom and Dad will come."

Pastor Roberts smiled warmly. "All right, you two, run along. Remember what we talked about today. I'll see you all tomorrow after lunch. May you allow God to direct your paths."

Jennifer stood, pushed her chair back, and leaned over to kiss Pastor Roberts on the cheek. Derek followed, moving his chair back and extending his hand.

"Thanks, Great Grandfather," he said, shaking his hand firmly.

As they walked toward the door, Derek felt a quiet weight in his chest, a mix of awe and gratitude. He realized it wasn't just the wisdom shared today that moved him; it was the sense of family he'd been missing, the connection to those who truly cared and would guide him in love. For the first time in a long while, he sensed his path might not be as uncertain as it had seemed.

The three left Pastor Roberts' room.

As they walked down the hall, Derek felt a quiet stirring in his heart. A sense of belonging he hadn't realized he'd been missing settled over him. It wasn't just the wisdom or the guidance—it was the family around him, the love and patience of those who truly cared. He glanced at Jennifer, noting the warmth in her presence, and he felt a peace he hadn't experienced in years.

Jody excused herself and slipped into another room, leaving Derek and Jennifer to exit the building. Jennifer told Derek that her mom and dad had wanted Pastor Roberts to move in with them when your grandparents died, but he said he was needed at the senior living facility.

The Harley thundered beneath them as they left the senior living center, the wind sweeping away words before they could even be spoken. Derek leaned into the rhythm of the road, the steady vibration of the bike grounding him, while behind him Jennifer's arms circled his waist, steady and warm. There was no need for conversation—the ride itself seemed to speak.

Derek felt strangely glad for her presence, the quiet strength of her nearness easing the weight he carried. Jennifer, for her part, found comfort in the steady way he handled the bike, a sense of safety and something more—something she couldn't quite name—settling in her heart.

When they pulled up to Jennifer's place, Derek cut the engine. The sudden stillness felt almost heavy after the roar of the ride. The silence pressed in, broken only by the ticking of the cooling motor. They removed their helmets, and Jennifer turned to him with a soft smile.

"Thank you for letting me be a part of today," she said

quietly. "Hearing your dream… it was something I won't forget."

Derek met her gaze, a little surprised by how much her words meant. "I'm glad you were there. It made today feel… lighter." He hesitated, then asked, "What do you think Pastor Roberts meant about coming back tomorrow?"

Jennifer slowly shifted from side to side. "I don't know. But I'm sure that whatever Pastor Roberts reveals will be enlightening."

Derek nodded and, with uncertainty, asked, "Would you like to come with me tomorrow? I'd love to have your company."

Jennifer's smile deepened, warm and sure. "I'd like that."

Jennifer led the way to her front door, and Derek followed, letting the quiet thoughts of the day linger. The ride, the visit with Pastor Roberts, the insights from his great-grandfather—all of it pressed gently on his mind.

Once inside, Jennifer hung up their coats and turned to Derek. "Do you want some coffee before you head home?"

"That would be nice," Derek replied.

As she prepared the coffee, Derek sat at the counter, watching her move with ease and warmth. He felt a rare sense of calm, as if the weight of everything had lightened somewhat.

Sitting together at the counter, the hum of conversation felt easy and natural.

"I still can't get over your dream," Jennifer said after a pause, stirring her coffee. "It's intense, but it makes sense when you consider what Pastor Roberts said."

Derek nodded, his thoughts drifting back to the masks, the darkness, the call to remove them. "Yeah. It's like I'm standing at the crossroads, but I don't even know which way to go yet."

Jennifer's eyes softened. "That's the thing about a Hill—you can't be told where it is. You have to see it to believe it. When the mask comes off and you take that one step, you'll begin to see the path."

Her words struck him, and what had seemed uncertain now seemed clearer. He sipped his coffee and felt the warmth spread not just from the cup, but from what he had experienced today. The ease of conversation was a quieting comfort.

As the evening approached, Derek stood and gathered his things. "Thanks for today, Jennifer. I… I really appreciated your company."

She smiled, a gentle glow in her eyes. "I'm glad I could be here with you. Tomorrow will be something. You'll see."

He nodded, a mixture of anticipation and trepidation stirring in his chest. Stepping out the door, he glanced back once, the lights from the house casting a soft glow, and he whispered a prayer under his breath:

"Jesus, guide my steps.

Show me the path You've set before me.

Help me to see clearly,

to take off the masks,

and to walk the road You've made straight."

The evening air enveloped him as he rode his bike, his heart lighter yet filled with quiet expectancy. Tomorrow felt like a threshold, and he knew that whatever awaited, he wouldn't face it alone.

Chapter 9

Into the Eternal

"The path may bend, the heart may falter, but in surrender, we find our way home." — Reflection

"To everything there is a season, and a time to every purpose under heaven." — Ecclesiastes 3:1

Derek did not have an eventful night. If he had a dream, he did not remember it. Morning slipped by as he moved through the quiet house, preparing to pick up Jennifer. His thoughts drifted back to something his great-grandfather had said: that the two of them were the only true blood relatives, and yet there was still a family bond between them all the same.

At the time, he hadn't given it much thought. But now it struck him that he had always called Greg and Diane "Uncle" and "Aunt" for as long as he could remember, though they weren't blood relatives. Jennifer, too, was not technically his cousin. And yet, the warmth of belonging had always been real. Perhaps that was what Great-grandfather meant: blood alone does not make family. Family was guidance, shared life, and holding to the same values. But he wondered why the thought surfaced now. He had always felt close to Jennifer growing up, yet now it stirred something deeper—something he wasn't quite ready to name.

Feelings he hadn't acknowledged before seemed to be taking shape, but he shrugged them off, unsure why they lingered.

His thoughts shifted back to Nancy.

The truth came with a shadow. Not everyone has known a real family. Nancy felt that way—he could hear it whenever she spoke of her mother, or the little she remembered of her father. There was a coldness there, like a door shut too soon. Perhaps that was why she held marriage at arm's length—why she kept God at a distance. If your first taste of family is loss and emptiness, why trust anything that claims to last?

Even so, Derek felt a new stirring. His time here was nearing an end; soon, he would return to the city. Decisions weighed on him about his future, about the life waiting beyond these quiet days.

One thing he knew: these past few days had changed him. His life had been altered, and that would affect both him and Nancy.

Derek packed his suitcase and called Nancy to let her know he would be returning late this evening. As he finished, his thoughts drifted back to her. He realized how much she had missed experiencing a real family. What little she remembered of her parents left a coldness in her mind. But Derek understood that blood alone did not make a family. Family was found in guidance, in sharing life, and in holding to the same values. That was why Christ spoke so often about family, and why God Himself calls His followers family. Perhaps that was part of Nancy's hesitation about marriage and even about believing in God. She did not understand what the Bible was saying about family and togetherness.

Derek left through the garage and paused for one last look at the Harley. Memories of Grandfather Dirk polishing it, then sitting back to admire it, came to him. He could almost hear Grandmother Melissa's cheerful voice: *"Are you going to spend all day out here? I like to see a bit of you too."* His grandfather's playful reply echoed in his mind: *"What did I ever do to deserve you?"* That light banter had been a part of their day. That simple exchange would always bring warmth to Derek's heart—a glimpse of the family he longed for.

Derek went through a checklist to ensure everything had been taken care of. Note to the cleaning lady, thanking her for the sandwich she had prepared—done.

He climbed into his car, pressed the automatic-close button, and watched the Harley disappear behind the closing door. He felt a mixture of gratitude, sadness, and purpose. He was glad he had come home, yet he knew it was time to return to the city. There were decisions he still had to make. But one thing was clear: the past few days had changed him, and that change would inevitably affect both him and Nancy.

Now focused, Derek drove toward Jennifer's house. Memories from their teenage years surfaced—how much they had enjoyed each other's company—and he realized that hadn't changed. Back then, with her braces, he hadn't really noticed her looks. But now, at five foot six, she was not only attractive; there was a presence about her—steady, content, deeply satisfied.

He was grateful she hadn't pressured him about the teaching position. The pay was far less than what he earned now, and his current job gave him the freedom he liked. For today, he set all that aside. He needed to see what his great-grandfather, Pastor Roberts, was being so mysterious about. And then he would discuss the teaching position with Jennifer.

When Derek pulled up to Jennifer's house, she was just locking her front door. She came down the steps with a warm smile and slipped into the passenger seat. That smile lingered in Derek's mind, making him strangely glad she was with him again.

As they drove, Jennifer's eyes fell on the suitcase in the

back seat. The car, not the Harley. Her heart tightened. She almost wished she hadn't noticed, but the truth pressed in all the same. He was leaving. She wanted to ask, but instead said gently, "So… you're not riding the Harley today?"

Derek shook his head. "No. I need to get back to the city. There are things I need to settle."

Jennifer nodded, keeping her gaze on the road ahead, though a quiet ache stirred inside her. She hadn't expected to feel this way—comfortable with him, safer than she'd felt in a long time. It unsettled her how natural it was, as if she belonged there beside him. And now, with the suitcase sitting between them like an unspoken truth, she feared it would be gone before it had a chance to become real.

As the silence stretched, Jennifer's thoughts turned inward. Am I the woman in his dream? The one without the mask, urging him to see clearly, to speak, to stand? She wanted to tell him outright, *Derek, take the step of faith. Say yes to the teaching position. That's where God is leading you.* But the words caught in her throat.

No… I can't pressure him, Jennifer thought, gripping her hands in her lap. *This is something he must see for himself. Jesus, it's in Your hands. Open his eyes, guide his steps. Use me if You will, but let it be Your work, not mine.*

The road stretched on in silence until Derek spoke again, his voice low but steady.

"After this day with Pastor Roberts is over… we need to talk."

Jennifer glanced at him, searching his face. His words left everything hanging—was he speaking of his decision, or something more? She couldn't tell. She only knew it mattered.

They pulled into the lot of the senior living facility, the building standing quiet under the midday sun. Derek shifted into the park, ready to step out, when Jennifer's phone buzzed in her hand. She glanced at the screen, her brow furrowing. For a moment, she hesitated, then answered.

"Hello?"

A pause, then her face went pale.

"Brad? …How did you get this number?" Her voice tightened, sharp and guarded. "I said all I need to say."

Without waiting for a reply, she ended the call, slipped the phone back into her purse, and shut it off.

Derek studied her, surprised. "Who was that, if I may ask?"

Jennifer forced a small breath, though her eyes didn't meet his. "Someone from my past."

The unease in her voice hung between them, and Derek caught the uncomfortable look shadowing her face. He wanted to ask more, but before he could, Jennifer opened her door.

"We should go. Pastor Roberts is waiting."

The moment settled like a question left unanswered as they stepped out and headed toward the entrance.

Pastor Roberts' Home – Senior Center

They arrived at the senior living facility, where the receptionist greeted them warmly.

"Pastor Roberts is expecting you," she said, her smile carrying a quiet understanding.

Derek and Jennifer walked down the quiet hallway until they reached Pastor Roberts' door. It was close, so Derek knocked. A moment later, Jody opened it, ushering them in.

Inside, Jennifer's parents, Greg and Diane, were already seated. Jody had arranged extra chairs in a half-moon shape, with a fresh pot of coffee set nearby. The atmosphere felt intimate, like a family gathering, yet with a solemn weight that hinted at the moment's significance.

Pastor Roberts sat in his usual chair, his eyes bright with a mixture of age and wisdom. He clasped his hands, taking a slow breath.

"Thank you, all, for coming," he began, his voice steady but carrying a gravity that immediately drew attention. The room grew quiet.

Pastor Roberts leaned back, looked toward heaven, and whispered, "Father, guide these words," his voice warm with gratitude.

"Your coming means more than you know. You see, this is how God views His family—we are all one, yet each of us carries a special quality that sets us apart. Greg, you were a steady friend. Dirk and I have both appreciated the kind of presence that anchors others in faith. Dependable. There are others who need your guidance, and God will use you."

Pastor Roberts turned to Diane. "Your quiet strength speaks volumes, often in a way that goes unnoticed. But God sees. Your patience, your nurturing, your faithfulness to those who have lost their way—all of it will bear fruit in ways you cannot yet see. Sometimes people overlook the profound impact a steady heart can have, but God never misses. You've carried burdens with grace, and He will honor that. Dirk told me how you helped steer him and Greg after losing Jenny, how you sat them down and talked about how loss affects us. Those moments mattered, Diane. They still matter, and they do not go unnoticed by God."

Jennifer's heart lifted as Pastor Roberts' gaze rested on her.

"Jennifer, you've grown in ways you might not fully recognize. Like Esther in the Bible, you may not see the full gift God has placed in you, but He does. You will face challenges as a school principal. Something unexpected is coming into your future. Don't be afraid. God is preparing you for such a time. The surrounding morality has shifted, but remember—Jesus walks with you. Keep the Hill as your place of strength and prayer. And He has provided a partner for your journey—someone who will walk beside you in unity."

Jennifer's mind briefly flickered back to the unexpected phone call from Brad earlier, a shadow of unease lingering despite her outward calm. She shook it away, focusing on Pastor Roberts' words. Her eyes met Derek's, and for a fleeting moment, a quiet question hung between them—unspoken, unresolved, yet impossible to ignore.

His eyes softened as he looked toward Jody.

"Jody, you've become like a daughter to me. You never

had a father to guide you, and I was honored that you looked to me as a grandfather figure. I rejoiced when you came to believe and follow Christ. You've been a joy to me, and not just me; I hear the same from many residents in this facility. Grow in your faith."

Finally, his gaze rested on Derek.

"And Derek, you carry a weight on your shoulders, but never forget—God didn't make a mistake in calling you. The dark forces will whisper that you cannot make a difference, but that's a lie. You may stumble, but so did Moses, so did Paul. What matters is that you rise again and keep walking forward. You know the decision you have to make. Sometimes we struggle even when we already know what we must do. Those two women in your dream gave you a clear choice: you cannot walk both paths. Derek, the Lord is asking you to trust Him with the step He's placed before you."

A silence settled over the room until Diane spoke softly.

"Roberts, this conversation sounds so final."

"It is," he replied gently. "People go through each day as if they have plenty of time. But do they? We never know what tomorrow may bring. That is why today matters. That is why I needed to speak now. Times are difficult, and they can leave us confused, making us wonder why this is happening."

Pastor Roberts lifted his hand and pointed to Derek, then to Jennifer. They both spoke almost in unison.

"We cannot always understand what God is doing, but we can always trust Him."

Pastor Roberts smiled warmly.

Most people never know when their time is ending. But I was given the privilege. Althea told me I am expected, and people are getting excited about my arrival. Most never meet someone like her, and many things are meant to remain a mystery until the right time. What matters is the message she delivered, not her presence.

He paused, letting his gaze sweep across the room before continuing.

Derek's eyes widened. That was the lady I met the other day I arrived here. She told me people were expecting you, Great-grandfather. I never knew what she meant. She shared some wise words with me, but no one seems to know her. And now that I hear you speak of her, the pieces have aligned—her presence, the message, the mystery.

Jody nodded thoughtfully. Over the years, we've had

people talk about Althea, but no one has been able to locate her.

Pastor Roberts smiled gently, a twinkle in his eye. Perhaps some things remain a mystery until the right time. What matters is the message she delivered, not her presence. I thought now was the perfect time to say what I needed to, given that Derek will leave soon.

Derek's eyes opened wide with surprise, having only mentioned his departure to Jennifer on their drive here.

I needed to share something important—it might sound like a lecture or a sermon, but I make no apologies. Christians talk about salvation, and that is a good thing. But do we really understand the gift we were given? When you examine the Old Testament and the tabernacle, you see how seriously God took sin, and that a price had to be paid. If we look deeply into our hearts, we see that Jesus conveyed that even our thoughts are abominations to the Heavenly Father. That does not contradict the Old Testament; it reinforces the idea that the heart is deceitful, and who can understand it? And when Jesus says He came to fulfill the law, He tells us the sacrifices were insufficient to pay the price for sin. Yet many Christians do not grasp that. We take sin lightly, except for those big sins. That is not what Jesus was conveying. Our minds, of course, deceive us. We want to believe that our families, friends, and those around us are okay. They have to be, don't they?

He let the words hang in the room for a moment, allowing each person to feel the weight of what he had just said.

Then his voice grew firmer, drawing attention to the craftiness of Satan.

Paul tells us our battle is not with flesh and blood, but with forces we cannot see. That is true, but let us not see Satan behind every misstep. Yes, we battle darkness, and no one looking at our world would deny that, but they don't understand it. Our own sinful hearts are responsible for much of what happens in the world, and when you feed the heart with more darkness, the darker it becomes. Pastor Roberts flicked through the pages of the Bible resting on his lap and read the apostle Paul's words: *"Set your mind on the things above, not on things on the earth."* He turned the pages again and read, *"Fix your thoughts on what is true, and honorable, and right, and pure."* We do not realize how important those words are.

Satan does. He is cunning. He knows how to influence culture on a massive scale. Our education system is not exempt— many young people leave college profoundly changed. Hollywood, films, the music industry—they prey on our emotions, shaping desires and perceptions. Television and the media are no different. Even churches are not immune. Many songs, if carefully examined, carry messages that stray from Scripture. Society, culture, and media—they shape minds, subtly guiding choices. And choices have consequences.

Pastor Roberts paused, letting the words hang in the room, heavy with significance. Look at 1 Kings 9. Solomon was warned: follow God's principles, and you will be blessed; pursue other gods, and suffering will follow. That warning was not only for King Solomon; it applies to nations, to believing people, and to every individual. God is holy. Scripture repeats it three times: Holy, holy, holy is the Lord God Almighty. Too often, we forget this. True holiness, true obedience, begins in our hearts, and it shapes everything around us.

He reached for a worn set of pages.

I want to read something Dirk wrote and entrusted to me, Pastor Roberts said, his voice steady yet weighty. He wrote of when he meets Jesus in heaven, standing before Him, and giving an account of his life. This is what he felt would happen.

Pastor Roberts took a deep breath and began to read. As he did, his hands trembled.

"The trumpet sounds. The angels stand at attention as

Christ enters and sits on the throne. No one needs to tell me what I must do. With shaking knees, I bow in awe. Even bowing seems insufficient. I drop face down on the floor; I try to hide my face. I attempt to hide myself by curling into a fetal position, but those piercing eyes observe everything, leaving nothing concealed. Although I hide from the throne, the glory blinds me. There is nowhere to hide.

I have never encountered anything like this before. My mind is overflowing, trying to grasp the righteousness, majesty, and glory. I thought I understood what Christ did for me on the cross, but I did not. I know how unworthy I am. All my failures flash before my face. It is so engulfing that I think it will swallow me. My weeping is overwhelming—I cannot stop. I see all the missed opportunities, the misspoken words that spewed from my mouth, and all the times I justified my actions, racing before my mind. I recall all the times I allowed my fear to stop me from doing what I knew Christ wanted me to do, and it feels like my heart will explode. He knows EVERYTHING. I cannot get my breath. My tears will not stop. My heart hurts. If I could die a thousand deaths, I would still experience nothing like this. Why did I listen to the wrong voices? Why did I allow myself to think those things would bring me peace? Why was I selfish? Why— Why—Why! 'Jesus, help me. Forgive me,' are the words that finally spring from deep inside me. The same words that gave me a new life when I repented and said I would follow Him. I knew I was saved, but these words are for my shame and for recognition of His holiness. In that moment, I fully know what Christ did for this sinner. At the very moment of judgment, I understand Christ's love. He wipes away all my tears. I am given a new life. I understand what Christ did on the Cross. He took my place. I thought I knew what salvation was. Now I truly know."

Pastor Roberts slipped the worn pages back into his Bible and looked slowly around the room, letting his gaze linger on Derek and Jennifer.

I want you to understand why I am sharing this with you today, he said, his voice quiet but filled with weight. There is much to do before Christ returns, and the world you live in will not understand your choices. You will face opposition not from casual believers, but from a world whose values stand in direct opposition to Christ's. His worldview contradicts the ways of the world.

He paused. The room seemed to hold its breath. Derek felt a quiet stirring in his chest—a mixture of awe, fear, and hope. Jennifer's fingers unconsciously tightened around her coffee cup, her thoughts mirroring his tension.

I want to remind you of the experiences you've walked through—the lessons, the challenges, the victories. Through them all, Jesus has walked with you. He carried your sins on the cross, and He can be trusted. Pastor Roberts repeated, "He can be trusted." So stand steadfast, even when the road feels hard, and let the certainty of His presence guide every step. What I share today is my encouragement to you.

Pastor Roberts looked at Greg. "We became closer friends over the years. You have much to offer others; don't cut yourself off. Others need what you can offer." He handed Greg a letter. "This is my last wishes."

Turning to Diane, he said, "You have lost much, but that loss has not deterred you from your faith. Christ will honor that. Your guidance to young mothers will be a blessing."

Pastor Roberts looked at Jody. "I remember the day you realized Christ had paid for your sins. The word 'sinner' is uncomfortable. People often say, 'Ask Jesus into your heart,' but they often miss the part about forgiveness. The holiness of God can be overlooked, as can His utter repulsion of sin. But Adam and Eve knew differently. That is why they hid. You declared you were a sinner saved by grace through faith. Take that truth, nurture your faith, and get involved so it will grow."

"Jennifer, your days ahead will be challenging. The morality of our society has shifted away from Christ's principles. What is good today would not have been good some years ago. Being a Christian principal will not be easy. I am thankful you have your Hill. Let it remain your place of strength and prayer. And God has a plan for you. You will not need to walk alone."

Jennifer, unnoticed by Derek, quickly glanced at him. She thought briefly about the unwanted phone call she had received from Brad. The voice had startled her, and though she had said all she needed to, the encounter left a strange, uncomfortable weight lingering at the edge of her awareness. She shook it off and focused on Pastor Roberts, but a small uneasiness remained.

Now Derek's great-grandfather paused. His voice was low, solemn, and deliberate.

"Derek—you've been given a choice, and it is no small thing. What you spoke of in your dream was not just a story; it was a mirror of your life. The broad way will call to you—it always does—but only one path leads to life." He leaned forward slightly. "And hear me now: this is bigger than you. Governments will grow more ungodly. The systems of this world are turning further from God every day. Darkness tightens its grip, and Satan himself knows his time is short. He will use every distraction, every counterfeit truth, and try to use every life around you to keep people from bowing to Christ.

"Yet God's Spirit is moving. He is working in hearts across the world, calling people out of sin, drawing them into His kingdom. Even in chaos, He is gathering His people, preparing His bride. He is calling you, Derek, to be a worker in His kingdom."

Pastor Roberts let the words sink in. "Derek, understand this: neutrality is not an option for any Christian. To delay is to decide. Either you will love Him or you will love the world. Either you stand with Christ, or the spirit of the age will sweep you away.

"And yet here is the hope: Jesus walks with those who are His. You will not face the fire alone. He has already shown you His love, and now He calls you to answer Him with love. Derek, do not fear or compromise, for it would rob you of the life God is offering. Choose Him, and stand steadfast, no matter what comes."

Pastor Roberts took a deep breath and paused, his hand pressing lightly against his chest. Jody quickly rushed over and checked his pulse, worry in her eyes. He looked up at her with steady eyes and warm concern and said, "I must finish this."

He took another slow breath, his voice softening. "One more thing I want to tell you, and then I'm done.

"My grandmother was taken as a slave when she was only twelve. By thirteen, she had my mother. When my mother and the owner's son fell in love, they ran away together. Eventually, he was forced to return home, and my mother, unable to raise me on her own, left me in a basket at a small country store.

"Some would see that as a tragedy—but I don't. I see it as God's grace, His hand upon my mother and upon me. It was an act of sacrifice, love, and faith. My mother trusted that God would guide the right people to find me. And He did.

"The family who found me was strong in their faith. They loved me as one of their own. That's what God does He turns pain into purpose and guides His followers with grace."

A quiet stillness filled the room. Everyone sat speechless, surprise written across their faces everyone except Greg. Diane glanced at her husband, realizing he already knew.

Greg nodded slightly, his voice calm but respectful. "I heard this years ago," he said softly. "But it wasn't my story to tell."

Pastor Roberts leaned back slightly, meeting each of their eyes. "I don't speak of this often, because the dark forces want to use such stories to divide us to make us see only the pain, to stir anger instead of healing. But God's story is different. Where the enemy tries to show bitterness, Christ plants redemption. Where darkness says, 'Remember what was taken,' Christ says, 'Look at what I've given.'

"Yes, life can be difficult. But I've learned something: Christ is stronger than any difficulty, past, present, or future. Satan wants you to live in the shadow of what went wrong or what goes wrong, because he knows it blinds us to what God is still doing. He wants us divided, focused on wounds that never heal. But Christ points to hope. His cross isn't just about forgiveness; it's about new beginnings every single day.

"The truth is, there is only one race the human race. A sinful human race. A race that Christ loves and died for. When God looks at people, He sees them all of them as lost sinners in need of rescue. That is why Christ came. Those sinners who are rescued by grace through faith begin to see things differently.

"Each of us is unique. Each of us has a role to play in Christ's kingdom. The world is selfish. It thinks only of its needs, desires, and wants.

"My work is finished, but yours must continue. Walk boldly in Christ's ways, love as He loves, and stand for truth even when it costs you. Face the darkness knowing Christ is with you, and let your life point to Him, for what you do in His name echoes far beyond what the world can see. Christ calls us to something greater. And remember this most important thing: we serve a risen Lord, and His sovereignty is summed up in what Joseph said about evil being done: '*You meant it for evil, but God meant it for good.*' Hold on to that belief, that assurance, and you can face whatever comes."

Pastor Roberts let the words hang in the room. Silence filled the space. For some, this was the first time they had even heard this story. It was the kind of silence that seemed to hold its breath, as if one could hear a pin drop. Every heart felt it. Every breath seemed too loud. Holiness itself seemed present. And somewhere in that Holiness, Derek wondered if Althea was standing nearby.

Pastor Roberts looked at Greg, his breathing slow but steady. "Greg," he said softly, "in my top dresser drawer is a large envelope with my will and last wishes, as we talked about."

Greg nodded, his voice quiet with emotion. "I will, Roberts."

Jody stood up slowly. "I need to go and get your pills," she said, her voice catching slightly as she stepped out of the room.

For a few moments, the room remained still. The late afternoon light fell across the floor, soft and golden. Pastor Roberts turned to Jennifer and Derek. "Would you please help me to bed?"

They arose, each taking an arm as they helped him from the chair and eased him into bed against the pillows. Once he was settled, he gave a faint smile. Greg and Diane remained nearby, quietly watching, aware that something sacred was unfolding, their hearts full but their words held back.

After a pause, Derek turned to Jennifer, his voice low and earnest. "Jennifer, I'm sorry I didn't tell you sooner, but I would like that teaching position if it's still being offered. I knew when you first offered it that it was what I needed to do. I put off the decision, fighting what I knew was right. If the position is still being offered, I'll gladly take it. But I'll need to go back to Washington to settle some affairs first."

Jennifer smiled, her eyes brightening with warmth. "I was hoping you'd take the position," she said. "I believed it was right, but I knew it had to be your decision."

Greg and Diane exchanged a quiet glance—relief and joy flickering in their eyes—but they stayed silent, letting the moment belong to Derek and Jennifer.

Pastor Roberts' face softened, peace settling over him. In his weakness, he said, "I'm glad you decided, Derek. Life will not be easy for either of you. And in the future, changes are coming. But God will guide you, and His grace will be enough."

He paused, his voice growing weaker. "There is something I want to tell you both." Derek and Jennifer drew closer. "The Lord told me I wouldn't see the next season. Derek, you've carried questions and doubts, but they were never meant to hold you back. They were meant to strengthen your faith. You've been placed where God wants you. It will not be easy, but His Spirit will go with you. Step forward, even when the path feels uncertain.

"And Jennifer… you've carried burdens far too long; they are not yours to carry alone. Your life matters. God has bigger plans for you, but you will not walk alone. You are part of His plan, more deeply than you realize. Your faithfulness has not gone unnoticed.

"Both of you have been chosen to continue what I began— not in the same way, but in the same Spirit. Truth and grace walk together. When you face the storms of life, go to the Hill. He will be there."

Pastor Roberts took a breath. "Now I am ready," he whispered, as if talking to some unseen presence. Then he tried to turn his head but was unable and said, "*My work is done. I fought the fight. I have finished the race.*" His words seemed to fade.

The room seemed transformed. The air itself felt alive with holiness.

Greg bowed his head, feeling the weight of God's presence. "God... I feel Your presence. It's more real than anything I've known."

Diane leaned close to Pastor Roberts and took his hand. "Tell my Jenny," she whispered. "We miss her, and we're looking forward to that wonderful reunion."

Jody, who had quietly entered the room unnoticed, kneeled beside the bed, tears glistening. "Grandfather... thank you for showing me what family really is," she said softly, reflecting on how he had guided her in healing her anger and showing her what love looked like.

Jennifer's eyes filled with tears. "Thank you, Pastor Roberts, for showing me that God loves me not because I'm like or unlike anyone else, but because I am still deeply loved—created in His image."

Derek bowed his head, feeling the depth of the moment. "How blessed I am for the gift I was given." Leaning closer to his great-grandfather, he whispered, "Tell my grandfather thanks for the journals; the rest, they know."

Derek looked up and saw Althea standing quietly at the head of the bed, and, in a mouthful of words of gratitude, he silently said, "Thank you for stirring for what I thought was lost."

Pastor Roberts smiled one last time, a breath of pure peace passing over him. "He's here," he whispered. "He's always been here."

Then, with a final, gentle exhale that seemed to mingle with eternity, Pastor Roberts was gone.

Silence filled the room, thick and holy. Each person felt it in their own way—Greg with reverence, Diane with tender sorrow, Jody with gratitude, Jennifer with peace beyond understanding, and Derek with a new depth of faith.

Outside, the world continued in its noise, unaware of the depth of what had taken place. But inside that room, heaven had touched earth, and those present knew they had experienced it.

Derek looked toward the window as golden light streamed in. "Thank you, Lord," he whispered.

Jennifer squeezed his hand. "He's home."

Derek nodded. "And now it's our turn to keep walking."

The four stood together, still, hearts full, the truth of Pastor Roberts' last words echoing softly in the room: "You meant it for evil, but God meant it for good."

Derek met Jennifer's eyes, a quiet understanding passing between them. No words were needed. In that moment, he knew what he must do.

The room stayed still, the weight of Pastor Roberts' words lingering in the air. Outside, the world continued its noise, but inside, a path had been cleared—one that would carry them forward, step by step. Derek understood that the quiet before the storm was itself a gift—a moment to steel his heart, anchor his faith, and prepare for the unseen challenges that lay ahead.

He inhaled deeply, feeling the weight of the calling settle over him like a mantle, heavy and holy. The room remained hushed, the silence almost sacred, as though the world itself were holding its breath, waiting watching to see what Derek would do next.

Look for the 4th Book:

The Hill: The Choice Within

Other Books by the Author

- *The Hill: Seasons of the Heart*, 2025

- *The Hill: The Journey Begins*, 2025

- *The Lie*, 2025

- *I Don't Want to Go to Heaven: Judgment Day*, 2024

- *Who is This God: Journey of Faith* (2nd Edition), 2023

For further information, contact the author:

Email: wjconfire@gmail.com

Website: https://www.waynejcoleman.com

About the Author

The Hill: Finding The Way

Wayne J. Coleman is an ordained minister with thirteen years of pastoral experience. He holds a B.A. from the University of Winnipeg, a B.R.S. from Mennonite Brethren Bible College (now Canadian Mennonite University) in Manitoba, and an M.Div. from Acadia Divinity College in Wolfville, Nova Scotia. Throughout his varied life, Wayne has served in the Canadian Military, worked as a miner in Thompson, Manitoba, and owned his own business—experiences that have shaped his understanding of resilience and faith.

Wayne is a dedicated author with a growing body of work. He has published three books in *The Hill* series, with the fourth on the way. He has also written seven children's stories and is the author of *The Lie, I Don't Want to Go to Heaven: Judgment Day*, and *Who Is This God: A Journey of Faith*. His writing reflects his passion for exploring truth, faith, and the human experience.

He is a proud father of two grown children, a grandfather of four grandchildren, and a grown stepson. When he is not writing, Wayne loves to explore new ideas and stories, which led him to his latest venture, *The Hill*, a compelling blend of truth and fiction that invites readers on a fresh adventure into the depths of faith and discovery. Guided by a lifelong curiosity and a desire to inspire, Wayne's work seeks to challenge, encourage, and illuminate the path toward understanding.

Wayne James Coleman

"Life has taken me down many roads: faith, service, and discovery. Each step has revealed that the true journey is not always where we expect it to be, but in how we respond to the truth we find along the way. It is in the quiet moments, the unexpected turns, and the stories we carry that we discover who we truly are. As I continue to write and explore, I remain committed to seeking understanding, embracing mystery, and sharing the hope that sustains us all."

www.ingramcontent.com/pod-product-compliance
Lightning Source LLC
Chambersburg PA
CBHW061103100726
47911CB00012B/370